The Book of Hrabal

The Book of Hrabal

Péter Esterházy

Translated by Judith Sollosy

Northwestern University Press
Evanston, Illinois

Hydra Books
Northwestern University Press
Evanston, Illinois 60208-4210

Originally published 1990 under the title *Hrabal Könyve* by
Magvető, Budapest. Copyright © 1991 by Residenz Verlag,
Salzburg and Vienna.

English translation first published in Great Britain by Quartet
Books Limited. Translation copyright © 1993 by Judith Sollosy.
Northwestern University Press edition published 1994 by arrange-
ment with Residenz Verlag and Quartet Books, Ltd. Hydra Books/
Northwestern University Press edition published 1995. All rights
reserved.

Printed in the United States of America

ISBN 0-8101-1199-3

Library of Congress Cataloging-in-Publication Data

Esterházy, Péter, 1950–
    [Hrabal könyve. English]
    The book of Hrabal / Péter Esterházy ; translated by Judith
Sollosy.
        p. cm.
    Originally published: Evanston, Ill. : Northwestern University
Press, 1994.
    ISBN 0-8101-1199-3 (paper : alk. paper)
    I. Sollosy, Judith. II. Title.
PH3241.E85H713 1995   95-30241
894'.51133—dc20   CIP

Te vocamus, quod sic plasmavisti hominem et nominem itidem vocamus, qui tamen debet praestare seipsum percipe hanc altercationem in corde nostro diabolicam, Domine! Et oculos sanctos Tuos in inopiam nostram conjicere non gravator, sed conspice postentum clam nobis abditum, in extis. . . accedit, quod allectationes nutriunt ipsum velut alece. Et ne nos inducas in tentationem, supplicamus ad vesperum, peccatum tamen ostium pulsat intratque domum et intrat prosus ad mensam. Amove ergo sartaginem igneam, quoa caro siccatur, name animal in me debile crebro.

We call upon Thee, who created man to be such as he is, and likewise call upon man, who is after all responsible for himself . . . wouldst Thou consider this, too, my Lord, this satanic back talk in our hearts! And do not restrain Thy holy eyes from beholding this wretchedness, and the monstrosity that dwells hidden in our innards, for it too contributes to this, it feeds upon temptation as if it were feeding on fish soup. And lead us not into temptation, we beseech Thee at nightfall, but sin comes knocking on our door, yea, even enters our room, advancing up to our very tables. Mayest Thou remove far that red-hot frying pan in which our flesh roasts, for the animal in us is so very frail.

from a medieval devotion
in Milán Fust, *The Story of My Wife*

The Chapter of Fidelity

'I am a Czechoslovakian, sir!' says the one.
The other slaps him and says, 'So what?'
Hrabal, *The Betrayal of Mirrors*

1

The two angels spoke to each other in the language of (what else?) angels. They had assumed the guise of young men; one of them was called Blaise, the other Gabriel, but everyone, including the Good Lord, just called him Cho-Cho.

'Look here, Cho-Cho, you'd better go and check out what in God's name, if you'll pardon the expression, they're up to down there . . . Straight to the point, minimum of fuss, but plenty of circumspection, you know how it is . . . free will and tact and all that jazz. And take someone along . . . You'll need him.'

'For a witness?'

'Are you pulling my leg, Cho-Cho, or what? You're an *azes ponem*, a wiseguy, eh? So stop it. And cut the crap. No need spelling it all out. What're you, a frustrated accountant? Don't you make me account for myself, you hear?'

These words (and it should surprise no one) did not shatter

the Cosmic Silence, words to which no stardust adheres, for angels do not speak the language of God, only that of the lesser orders, the language of men, animals and plants, pebbles, the language of crystals, the language of molecules and atoms – but hold it! What's with the lists again? You can't go hacking the world into smaller and smaller units, we're bursting with energy, the part no longer smaller than the whole, a cosmic dance, a new link between form and emptiness, and oh! there is *inter*course between space and time; instead of existence and action we must now speak of existential and active tendencies; up front and behind, the World curves in upon itself, its head where its ass ought to be, and vice versa, and I wouldn't be surprised if smack dab in the centre of the nucleus, there crouched the Good Lord summoned by hosannas of leptons. In short, the angels speak Greek, too, are familiar with the nature of secret military codes, and (needless to say) they also know a thing or two about finite algebras. And so the Lord is bound to address them in the language of his angels.

Come to think of it, the Good Lord can converse in his own language only with himself, seeing how there's nobody greater than the Lord, because if there were, he'd be the Lord, and for all I know, things may already have come to this comical pass. In short, God's language is the language of self-love (i.e., of silence, but hush). And that's just fine. Because if it should turn out that the Lord did not love himself, we'd be in a pretty pickle, for in that case, he'd make double sure that we should have no reason to take ourselves into our own good graces either. And in our turn, we, the children of God, would double up on the revenge; everything would soon come to an end in the blinking of an eye, a graceful, spine-chilling blink. But it seems that ('just like the ocean') the Good Lord possesses a nature that is epic.

We find eloquent, cogent and awesome accounts of the

language of angels in the apocryphal literature of the third century. Especially stunning is the cruel and third-rate debate between Archangel Michael and Seth, the 'surviving son' ('mourn for six days only, etc.'), and the most complete example is in *Apocalypses Apocryphae*, pp. 24–33, G. Olms, Hildescheim, 1966. Barthes comments wittily, 'As if on his deathbed Wittgenstein had returned to the *Tractatus*. Friends, this is the language of angels, and not of victory.'

We wave this off with good reason: mere analogies.

The man on the street is much more practical. Who are they? Whose hide are they after? Could it be mine? That's how it goes, what is real is replaced by innocence, innocence by lurking malevolence, malevolence by fear. And since you can't live in fear forever, and the waiting cars drive off after a while, fear is replaced by innocence once again. This is the latter-day, *soft* version of the dictatorship of the proletariat.

At first, the two taciturn young men inside the Lada with the AI (state) licence plate did not create a stir in the neighbourhood. This little corner of the city still preserved, if not the trace or the remnant, then the shadow . . . i.e., it did not even preserve, it merely bore the imprint of the distant memory of the former settlement, a sort of village that had stood before it was absorbed by the metropolis in the late twenties.

But now, the vague shadows of the former village's reflexes suddenly surfaced: the movement, the pain of an amputated leg, more than nothing, less than custom (not to mention tradition). You couldn't call it a surburb, though it fell at some distance from the city centre; those who lived here went *into* town, which involved planning, took determination, called for a decision. There was a main street lined with plane trees and poplars, and mostly cottages with gardens, not villas, they were more modest or lowly than that, and more functional; 'family homes' is the name of this style-less, practical sort of dwelling; the neighbourhood had been called a 'garden city' as well as a resort area, for it once had a wordly strip along the Danube – bathhouses, beach, water-front activities. But all of that gradually phased out due in part to the pollution of the river, in part to the change in recreational trends; the waterfront activities were replaced by tennis or nothing at all, while the bathers moved down to the public pool near the main street (which instantly necessitated modernization, to wit, it was closed down, though later reopened again).

There was a café of sorts and two rival taverns, which everyone called by their old names, the Beerhall and the Kondász (old man Kondász was still kicking, he had his own table in the corner and ordered beer by the pint, an unknown quantity for the succession of ever new barkeepers, *it's a pitcher and a dash, son*! half a litre plus the missing 'dash' to make it a pint, until they got fed up and compromised on a full pitcher); there was also a beauty parlour, a boutique, formerly a shoe repair shop, and there were the natives, and there were the newcomers. Everyone did not know everyone else, the way custom and propriety dictates in a village, but there was a shared knowledge of things, of the fact that time passes – which may have meant no more than that there was a public opinion making itself felt through the usual channels, the market, the post office (via the mailman), the butcher's shop, the square in front of the church.

I find inordinate satisfaction in seeing this layering of time, from pint to pitcher, from malt beer allotments to new mothers to labour unions dues and beyond, when I see that the present cannot devour everything else, everything that is not itself, but is, in fact, the past and the future. Mine is a joy begotten by the sight of organic growth, a deification of

4

nature, perhaps, which might be silly, of course, and is clearly fraught with unpleasant consequences. Whenever I discover nature, which is divine, in something man-made, I consider it good and fitting. Is this jumbling of the good and fitting reality or innocence, lurking malevolence, or fear? Whatever it is, sooner or later, we must all pay the price.

The first moment in time is identical with the moment of Creation, writes Saint Augustine. Remarks about the nature of time are irresponsible, you can't defend them, the sentences are so thoroughly soaked in time, they slop about instead of splashing merrily, at best they paddle about, you could squeeze time out of them like old, tepid water from a wet dishrag. That's how things stand. Who can account for two hours? Two hours have gone by since the butter-yellow Lada had pulled slowly and tentatively into this unpaved side street off the main street across from the public pool. In the house, which the strangers have been staking out for the past two hours, there lived a family (this was a family house!), a married couple with three children, the woman's name was Anna, and the man was a writer.

Along the fence facing the side street rose a dense hedge, or rather, the hedge itself constituted the fence, and it wasn't even a hedge, but a thicket of unpruned bushes and saplings; this neglect was the hedge, it accounted for its density. The writer enjoyed the shelter, the sense of security it provided. Naturally, the hedge constituted no hindrance to the sight of the two angels, and when the lowly music of the unoiled hinges announced the opening of the front door and the lady of the house emerged, they were afforded a full view. They had been waiting. And then Cho-Cho spoke thus: 'Just look at that ass!'

Blaise blushed, a rosy hue on the low horizon, wind in the

offing? And the angelic lashes, butterfly wings weighing a ton, fluttered.

'What a profanity, oh, my brother, what a vile word, and how beautiful!' Cho-Cho sniffed, this sudden summertime chill was treacherous, it could mean a bad cold. The woman stretched and moaned softly, as if it was morning, and she, alone.

2

'I love those few moments before seven in the evening when I can polish the lamp cylinders with a rag and a crumpled copy of *National Politics*.' Anna loved those few moments before seven in the evening when she could step outside, alone at last, even if only for a few seconds; she stretched lazily, how else, as if it was morning, and she, alone, listening to the triple call of the thrush, few-few, futile-few, call-*addio*-few . . . 'I'm cricking and cracking.'

She liked not having anyone at her side, for she always had someone at her side, and she, too, was always at someone's side. You could hardly call this an evening's walk, it was more like an evening's leg-stretch, a few steps, no more: she ducked outside for a breath of fresh air, sighed once or twice, whistled a bit, and that was that. She whistled beautifully, as if she were singing alto, mostly Sonny Boy Williamson blues. This old black man was her current favourite, this Sonny Boy.

Weary of the daily ritual of phone talks with her father, she would at times amuse herself by imagining her father as Sonny Boy, that skin-and-bones stray dog, or rather, the other way around, Sonny Boy as her father. Kisses, kisses, everybody, I bring the sizzling-hot kisses of the sun for everybody. 'Hello, dad.' And she began to whistle, and Sonny Boy to grin, yeh, fellas, this here is my li'l gal, she's got music in her blood, oh yeh, a natural! What else did you expect? Sunny Girl, sweet and sad, any news of your ma?

'Are you whistling, is that you whistling?' Her realer than real father rasped testily, redundantly, meaning, was that whistling, and if so, was it hers?

'Oh, daddy, what an idea.'

'All right, child, don't get upset now.' You could sense that he knew the truth and was glad of the chance to be offended.

In that classic twilight – as the French say, that time between the dog and the wolf (I learned that one from Tsvetayeva, *entre le chien et le loup*) – solid blocks of yellow light poured forth from the windows, the house was studded with blocks of speckled gold, the flickering yellow light 'which casts a deep shadow, and makes you step lightly, dreamily'.

And so, Anna stepped lightly and dreamily, at peace; in the house, a great, confused hubbub, that's what she'd left behind, soon she'd have to feed them, too, and though the children set the table, they liked her *serving*, and she liked feeding them ('I love those glowing lamps of mine, in their light I carry plates and cutlery to the table, newspapers and books open up; I love hands in lamplight, the way they rest on the tablecloth, detached human hands in whose calligraphy is written the character of the person to whom the hand belongs . . .'), nor was it always so quiet out here, soon the seven o'clock bus would be coming, the six-forty-five, actually, late as usual, it was a Hungarian bus, with the windows of the houses rattling, one after the other, a tremor sweeping down main street, but here in the twilight zone between inside and outside, where the whistling woman stood, all was quiet a few moments before seven.

At this hour she even loved the flaws in objects; glancing up at the black sky she loved the sag in the eaves, the cracked and crumbling stucco, the advanced rust of the garden gate, loved everything that in the daylight she saw as a blemish, as yet another encroachment of evil, another assault by the decaying world that surrounded them and that she vowed to fight unto her dying breath, and she could not, she would not understand the writer, who was so fond of contemplating 'the hysterical refinement of cracks' or that 'ongoing drama skulking in the inner chamber' produced by a piece of plaster that for years now, incredibly, has been teetering on the brink of falling but has not done so, or the way he has interdicted the liquidation of cobwebs in his room, insisting on their inadulterated beauty, no, she did not want to understand this ambivalent glorification of decay, anarchy, confusion, chaos; but now she saw all this not as evil, but as idiosyncratic, the unique distinguishing marks of her life, there are our cracks and our rust, and this, my quarter of an hour, the fifteen minutes when the air cooled down with unexpected rapidity, it was no longer summer, and this, too, she loved, the way something could point out the passage of time with such tact, consideration, gentleness.

She also loved the passage of time. She was not afraid of it yet.

On the south-east corner of the house was a protrusion, a hump, a lump, originally an open terrace, where her husband worked now. If she peeped in through the window, cautiously, she would see the same thing, always, and as always, well nigh twenty years now, a passionate feeling would overcome her, so that she would groan, bend into it, playing, for herself, as if on stage; it was not salutary for anyone to catch sight of her now (except for the one she was playing for), as for instance her children, who occasionally did.

'Why are you touching yourself, Anna? Have you got a tummy ache, Anna?' The children called her Anna, though lately the oldest had started to say mama, she said the word with evident delight, mama.

Her husband was sitting behind an enormous desk. 'If,' he would instruct a child at the appropriate age, 'if this flat-top superstructureless late-Baroque desk, so popular in the eighteenth century, has four legs, and, don't suspect any tricks here, if among the copper fittings and mountings so abundantly covering the curved legs, if among the gilt copper acanthus leaves enclosing the spiral tips of the legs (the ornaments emphasize the structure of the desk and augment its formal and colouristic wealth), if there leans forward on each desk-leg one partially unclad lady, and if we may count two titties per lady, what's the total number of titties in this room, time's up!'

Over the years, each child had his or her own way of being intimidated by the father (and the father by the child). From the oldest down, respectively, this is what they replied:

'Eight.'

'What do you mean?'

'Infinite.'

Eight, the older girl, ran out of the room at once, and refused to talk to her father until nightfall. *What do you mean*, the son, sneaked back into the room later when it was empty, and whispered, 'Never you mind,' to the cool copper mounds he was caressing. The little one, the little *infinite* girl, stared back at him so openly and brazenly that her father finally couldn't stand it and yelled at her to beat it, and a great silence ensued.

At night, when he emerged from his lair, more romantically: his cave, he was hunched over, weary, like a miner; great shadows overcast his face, one eye smaller than the other, his eyelid tremulous, as if he were stuttering, or shivering, or blinking... 'There he stood in the shadow of the doorway, his white cuffs betraying the day's exhaustion, those two cuffs were practically down to his knees, he had piled so many cares and worries upon his shoulders in the course of the day that he always shrank four inches or more . . . And each night we stood under the bright pull-down lamp, its green shade big enough for us both to fit under, under that umbrella-sized shade, there we stood in the shower of hissing oil-lamp light, I had one arm around his waist, the other stroking the back of his neck, his eyes were closed, he took deep breaths, and when he calmed down, he took me by the waist; it looked like we were about to launch into some ballroom dance, but it was much more than that, a purifying bath, and he whispered into my ear all that had happened to him that day (for fantastic things would happen to him at his desk, he could tell only a fraction of it to his wife, nor was he able to set much more down on paper), and I kept caressing him, each movement of my hand smoothed away another wrinkle, then he caressed my tumbling hair, he had let it down, I kept pulling the porcelain light fixture lower, it was thickly festooned all around with coral and coloured glass beads strung together, all those jingalings tinkling close to our ears, like so many tin trinkets and baubles around a belly-dancer's hips; at times I had the sensation that the big pull-down lamp was a glass bell crunched down over both our heads, down to our ears, a hat bedecked with a shower of cut-glass icicles . . . I chased the last wrinkle from his brow, back somewhere into his scalp or behind his ear, and he opened his eyes, stood up straight, his cuffs back at waist level, he looked at me, suspicious and shy, and when I smiled and nodded, he smiled, too, then, with eyes averted, sat down to the table, gathered up his courage, and raised his eyes to me, and I, mine, to him . . .'

Anna shuddered in the evening cool. She forced herself not

to look in at the window. 'And I was aware that I was his greatest care, that he lugged me on his back in an invisible and yet concrete rucksack, one that was getting heavier and heavier by the day.'

Few-few, futile-few, call-*addio*-few . . .

3

To write about *something* – what does that amount to? Nothing. Sheer nonsense, the unity of form and content, the proof of the pudding, social progress, mastery of nature, union dues. The writer was supposed to write about Hrabal. Bohumil Hrabal, a Czech. Seventy-five years old. Prose. A name to be reckoned with. Hašek's vicar on earth. All numbers greater than fifty and divisible by five, and seventy-five is one of them, send littérateurs into a peculiar frenzy, they all get steamed up, you might say, and, most likely in order to allay their well-founded pangs of conscience, they set about tacking together stormily festive writings, or else by hook or by crook, manage to persuade others to do so.

A low-grade temptation is not the real thing. True temptation is first-rate and custom-made. It is a challenge, a trial of strength aimed at the very heart of self-esteem and at the (mostly suppressed) impulse toward asceticism. A clever invention. To make a long story short, the writer considered Bohumil Hrabal a literary giant. According to a popular joke, to be born a Hungarian, or more generally, an East- or Central- or East-Central European is a piece of bad luck. But according to this man Hrabal, or so the writer felt, this wasn't so, it wasn't bad luck, it was downright tragic, to be born here was tragic, even worse, it was comic. It was the stuff of drama. Of course, this was the same drama as any place else on earth, only the conditions for realizing this were far better here, the conditions were more obliging, and stood as constant reminders of the fact. This was why the Danube was so close to heaven. I will disregard here the relation of the perceiver to the perceived . . . Likewise, I will disregard this latent Central-European arrogance . . . What's this closeness to heaven? Let's not kids ourselves.

The work was rough going, but then, you could say that it always was rough going; whatever was going was rough, because if it weren't that, then presumably it wouldn't be going either, for whatever was going wouldn't be 'it'. Oh, let's drop it; figure it out for yourself.

The writer, it may be said, knew the fringes of the city quite well, the language, the rules, but it wouldn't be right to consider him plebeian. No. Hungarian literature has not done right by its plebeian traditions, I regret to say. On the one hand, the writer felt he understood Hrabal very well, and perhaps it wasn't entirely vainglorious to say so; he also observed that they were quite dissimilar. Dissimilar from head to toe. As different as two eggs. But this was just it: the writer was enabled to contemplate his own otherness, his strangeness. More precisely: at the moment, *this* particular strangeness. This might even merit the name of ambition. He was trying out, testing this strangeness, which his Czech colleague had brought out in him, testing it, which also meant looking for the familiar in everything; or to put it the other way around, he was only interested in all this to the extent that he could make good use of it, that's right, to the degree that it enhanced his productivity. The writer was the kind who, given the choice between life and literature, would choose literature at the drop of a hat, because he thought, he firmly believed, that literature was his life. The facts of life were not the facts of literature. But the truths of life were the truths of literature. This is what he professed, and he was not ashamed to own up to it, although (let me hasten to add), he was not proud of it, either.

Anna lived the simple life of literary widows.

Sometimes, when the writer did not speak all day and just sat in his room, Anna did not dare to look in, for he would make the most awful faces, snarling and that sort of thing. He even chewed his nails, which Anna detested, it was a bit much, from a man of forty. (But at least this was *action*; Hungarians hold action in high regard, meaning exclusively physical labour, so that a thinker thinking, or a writer writing does not necessarily merit attention, unless said thinker or writer happens to plant trees as community work, let's say – now that would be action. In which case the benefit to literature would be the shade the tree provided for the reader . . .) At times he gnawed the end of his pen, like some rodent. The writer clung to his pens with superstitious tenacity. He used to have a Parker, which he handled so much that he just about dented it; he lost it on a commuter train. (For Anna, 'Parker' had another meaning: she thought of the great Charlie, the 'Bird' . . . I might add that Charlie Parker lost several saxophones in the subway.)

The writer sat all day behind his enormous desk (that's why he was a writer), and spitefully handled and shuffled and fondled his slips of paper, his scraps, so that his desktop resembled a landscape, a desolate Tuscan downs, a habitable desert, a comfy, cosy spatial segment from a Tarkovsky movie; in other words, it was rather awesome, jam-packed, always full of incredible amounts of *material* lying in heaps, hills and dales, mounds, crumpled envelopes, manuscript pages, newspaper clippings, coloured felt pens, chestnuts, contracts, scribbles, expired passport applications, bus tickets, pencils, notebooks, deadline calendars, love letters (the minefields of expired love letters), paper clips, candy wrappers, annotations, books, letters, one enormous, humongous, dappled shambles – inner order, and all of it layered, standing in several layers, sandwich-like, complete with tunnels, secret deep drill-holes; one level held letters that had gone unanswered for two months, another those that in another two months will have gone unanswered for two months. The writer had a friend whose desk – the exact opposite of his – was a serene, flat expanse, clean manuscripts, neatly stacked, two pens. Only right angles on that desktop. Without work, there is neither bread nor geometry, Euclid supposedly said. And also that there is no royal road to geometry. Then he had another friend who did not even have a permanent writing desk; he wrote in his lap. Royal road?

It happened more and more that Anna dreamt of Hrabal. She kept quiet about this because her husband should have been the one doing the dreaming. He was having trouble. She could see that. But she pretended not to notice. However, she had to be aware of precisely the right moment when she should acknowledge that she knew he was having trouble. For if it was too soon, the charge flung at her head would be lack of confidence in him, if too late, neglect. He kept getting stuck. Temporarily, of course. He couldn't think of anything, he claimed, though that's an exaggeration, but ideas, original ideas, none, or once in a blue moon – it is to be feared that the writer was even proud of this – and anyway, he had nothing to say, only his books did. 'Come on, dear, save that for the reporters.'

It happened one morning that Anna wanted to endear herself by a gift sentence – 'It's likely to be a scorcher' – she knew the writer liked that sort of thing, the rare locution, or the irregular forms of certain verbs. In the matter of exhortations to housework, a thousand threats meant less to him than one well-worded admonishment such as, 'Hey, babe, make the bed you *lay* in', which worked not because of the heartiness of its tone, but because of that lay. If he reprimanded his *what do you mean* son for insolence, and the latter replied, although he had indeed been insolent, that he wasn't being insolent, his father began to shout at him; if, on the other hand, the boy replied in part truthfully and in part with subtlety that he had not *intended* to be insolent, then his father would leap up, leave everything, all pedagogic principles, behind, to run and brag to Anna about his son's refined style.

'What are you saying?! . . . a scorcher . . . what? I can't be expected to live this this.'

Anna nodded. 'No, I guess you really can't work in this heat.'

A mistake. Face contorted, the writer began to stamp his feet, a temper tantrum, his working was not a matter of will, it didn't depend on the sun or the rain, no, and the least he could expect was not to be bothered with weather trivia, and that he would indeed be surprised if his wife not only acknowledged his being at the mercy of his work but would, if only in her own way, appreciate . . .

'It's all right, pet.'

The writer rushed off in a tizzy, and Anna was again amazed by all the energy he could muster if he felt like it, for all sorts of superfluous things, in this case grimaces, wild gesticulations, growls, severe muscular spasms – patiently elaborated! Flaubert! – all meant to signal that this whole thing, this insignificant little tête-à-tête, in which doubtless he too had a role, was solely and entirely her fault; she had brought it about, and it was because of her that he had to leave now, and *waste his time* playing soccer at the nearby beach, instead of making himself available in the workshop of his great genius . . . 'Could it be that at these times he really forgets that for years now he's been spending every Sunday morning on the beach? . . . What a clown. And is this part and parcel of his being a writer, or am I simply unlucky? Tell me, Bohumil, what do you think?'

Hrabal saturated them through and through. They were up to their ears in Hrabal, who, no longer a mere human, became a way of life for them; they sucked him dry, spoke his sentences, copied the gestures of his heroes. Hrabal peeked at them from every nook and cranny – except there was not enough joy in this, even though theoretically it should have been a source of joy. Had they dissolved in Hrabal? Let's not exaggerate. They had merely fallen in love with him. For the Bólyais, the infinitely distant clearly is more erotic than for Euclid, Professor Surányi had said (or rather, his son, who is also Professor Surányi). Yes, indeed, we're stuck with a triangle, the sum of whose angles, under terrestrial circumstances, is a hundred and eighty degrees.

An afterthought: are all sons of Professor Surányi Professor Surányi? How's that, Bohumil?

4

'Yahweh calling, Yahweh calling. Angelus, can you read me.'

'Angelus calling. Angelus calling Yahweh. Yahweh, can you read me.'

'Look, Cho-Cho, what in good grief is going on?'

'No grief so far, Lord.'

'Cho-Cho. I'll let that pass without comment. But I will remark, *en passant*, that this was a pun, poor as it was, while puns, no matter how brilliant, are Satan's handiwork. But let it go. I don't want to be reminded of that man. Any results yet?'

'Nothing's happened yet, Lord.'

'Well, see that it does, bungler! Not to say *meshugge* . . .'

'Excuse me for making excuses, Lord, Lord of Lords, God of Gods, King of Kings, whose glory will shine forth through all time, whose name is hallowed and all that . . . But you know how it is, Big Boss . . . The machine has been set in motion, as you know, while the Creator rests . . .'

'For God's sakes, Cho-Cho, old buddy, for God's sakes . . . Where is your sense of proportion? If I told you once, I told you a thousand times, there's nothing like the golden mean . . .'

'Language seeks truth, Lord, and therefore cannot possess it. Language is dual in nature, like its tutelary deity Hermes, mixing the true and the false. It is obscure, for it blends light and dark.'

'Kiss my arse. Over and out.'

Like an enormous storm did silence rage inside the Lada. The nineteenth-century author Camillus Gabriel Tura (possibly the only one Nietzsche, and I realize this is a big word, *trusted*) puts it so well in his utterly charming and cheeky little book on Plotinus (Verlag der Durr'schen Buchhandlung, Leipzig, 1870): ultimate truth is beyond language. Language exists in a border region, on the turf of 'as if' – just like human beings. There is no grief, the angel reported, and this attitude, no two ways about it, supports the view expressed by Themen, a student of Empedocles (I call him Gabe, a charming man, something of a rarity these days; my wife likes him, too, due in no small measure to the young man's auburn locks, hypnotic smile and flashing teeth); according to him angels are made of absence and are fallibly perfect, and oh yes, they are gorgeous beings in a full state of grace who chatter weightlessly under an overcast sky, while feeding on the words of those who come from the world of humans, which, when they see them, sound strangely on the tongue. Steal the raisins off the sweet stuff of tragedy, that's what they would have liked! Naturally, grief was already on the way, from two directions at once, as it always – or almost always – happens in a marriage, not as a storm cloud, but as a fine drizzle of particles, like mist or sawdust or raisins, and yet all at once.

The two angels sat motionless in the Lada which was made in the Soviet Union on the basis of an old Fiat licence. Like a gold tiara, the gear-shift lever emitted flashes of yellow and purple light. Someone hurrying to the Kondász tavern now, or leisurely climbing the fence around the public pool – the writer, for one, chastised his children if they did *not* climb over the fence (i.e., if they paid their way in) – in short, a passer-by would not have known how to account for the confusion in the heart, the strange impulse to walk faster, the dread that urged him to scram.

Oh, should we question Life, or History?

It would appear that the flashing light did not emit a dread of the infinite, or the oft-sung dread of angels, but merely that of history. To put it briefly, Hungary in 1988 was not a nation living in fear. It was a nation living in uncertainty – its future was uncertain, its present was uncertain, even its past was uncertain.

People were not governed by wisdom, faith, philosophy or the relentless laws of economics, no; society did not attempt to find its bearings in the world, the nation, or even in itself according to such things, it did not draw its conclusions from these, nor did it fashion or attempt to fashion life in accordance with said conclusions. It took to reading signs instead, of which superstition, gossip and custom were the potent vehicles. Being unstructured by their very nature, signs could thus simultaneously recall primitive communal rites, the fireside fantasies of our ancestors that substituted for reality and created reality, too, as well as the vapid topicality of a night-club comic. The utility of signs dissolved the difference between ritual and cabaret; at the most, and quite unintentionally, at times it lent the superficial a seriously ironic air, or else mistook the primitive for the sublimely serious.

For instance, until very recently, fortune-telling from bones was a widespread practice in this country.

In spite of all the dramatic turnabouts of Church history, the cross remained the most authentic and effective emblem of Christianity – the cross, and not the burning stake, the thumbscrew or the papal tiara. There must have been a time, I guess, when socialism too could have been served by some symbol that 'pointed the way', some kind of social emblem, such as the pegs marking the new boundaries after the redistribution of land. For nowadays its symbol is more likely a day in the life of Ivan Denisovitch, the Gulag, a curtained car gliding noiselessly from victim to victim in the night darkened by blood. (I will leave God and freedom out of this, for now.)

The signs (the signs of signs) have lost some of their severity by now; on Channel One you can see a critical look at Stalin, in living colour, soft porn on Channel Two, and the curtained cars are no longer curtained (so that when we see a car without curtains, for they are the only kind to be seen, we don't know what to think, and so we've got ourselves a problem!)

It wasn't really a good sign, Anna's father-in-law was fond of saying, to have people stand around your car, with wild tongues of flame licking at the sky from the centre of the crowd. By the time it got noticed, by the time it was impossible not to notice, the neighbourhood could not have seen a good sign in the presence of the two inquistive men in the car with the government licence plate. Regardless of ethnic origin, religion, political conviction or sex, this country has been thoroughly thrashed, you might say, more than once. Spanked. (By whom? It hardly matters. Small country, one large mob.) Thrashed like a child, it's been; thrashed and spanked – reprimanded, scolded. That's how people usually talk about these things, like children: 'That same night the men were taken to the council building, where they were waiting for the special police from Budapest to show up, and then they were thrashed real bad, some got separated livers, that's when my husband started stammering, and my brother-in-law, Feri, he lost his manhood, he's been impotent ever since . . . Yes, they got a thorough thrashing.'

If, for instance, we were to count how many among Anna's and the writer's parents and grandparents were beaten by state forces, say since 1919 (to obtain a 'more historical' perspective than, say, since 1945), and if we count as a beating the severe police chastisement suffered by the writer's mother in 1957 (shadow punches thrown, being called a whore – a still-life with two spiteful, tired men in a little grey room), we'd end up with six Hungarian individuals who were beaten out of a possible twelve (one parent, and two grandparents on each side), which makes fifty per cent. So then, there are some who were beaten, and some who were not. They beat up everyone, every family; there is no street, no house in Hungary they did not hit (and this assumption is strengthened by the fact that in general, the beaters were also beaten, which does not mean that the reverse was also true, that the beaten also gave out beatings . . . There were some who hit back, but that is something else. For example, the writer's mother, who was so frightened by shock troops that she reacted by clocking the nearest one, which triggered a storm of swearing. 'I was never in my life so happy to be called a *whore*, son . . . To be a living whore.') If this much horror and infamy was visited upon one family ('Your uncle was executed today'), then how many went down in all? And who keeps count? I do, said the writer, resolved to be emotional, for it was his lot to recall everything and everyone; his mother's memory was in his keeping, and so was his father's, whether he wanted it or not, and his brother's, all . . . Anna was making faces, aren't you taking on too much, my precious?

The gold and purple gemstone flash of the gear-shift lever went out. The two men exchanged a gentle look. For the skin of angels is as delicate as soap bubbles. From the garden came Anna's whistling; she kept jabbing at one of Ray C. Sartorius's lesser-known numbers, which, in the late twenties, and I'm not exaggerating, drove New Orleans wild. (Ray C. is known as the 'Younger Sartorius'; his relationship with his older brother, for reputedly artistic reasons, was none too good, the brothers were not only jealous of each other, but hated each other's *tone*, the older ran with Bessie Smith, Queen of the Blues – see 'Empty Bed Blues'. ' "As if" was not in his vocabulary,' wrote the critics, perhaps partly in reference to his relationship.) 'That Ancient Celtic Sorrow on Your Face and Those Fabulous Tits' was the full title of a number Anna was whistling; it had emerged (possibly because of the lyrics?) expressly as an anthem of sorts, a kind of emancipation blues for housewives; the women took to the streets, they say, and danced and laughed, and twirled their bras like slings.

5

'Bohumil, love, how was that scene when your mother had her cascading, intoxicating lager-yellow mane cut off, and your father came running from the office that had a sign: "Where the beer is good and frothsome, drink a pint and then some", the three members of the society for urban beautification hard on his heels, and your father, the No. 3 drafting pen clenched between trembling fingers, asked, "Where is all your hair?". "There," said your mother, leaning her bicycle against the wall, and she lifted the top of the baggage rack, and handed over the two heavy braids of hair. Your father, Frantzin, slipped the pen behind his ear, pondered your mother's defunct locks, and put them down on a bench. Then he wrenched the pump off the frame of your mother's bike.

' "My inners are inflated enough," I offered, laying expert fingers on the tyres.

'But Frantzin unscrewed the rubber hose from the pump.

' "There's nothing wrong with the pump either," I pressed on, uncomprehending.

'At that, Frantzin lurched at me, laid me on his knee, pulled up my skirt, and thrashed my bottom, and in my astonishment all I could think was: did I have clean underwear on, had I washed properly? And was I exposed enough? Frantzin continued thrashing me, and the bicyclists nodded in approval, and the three females from the society for urban beautification looked on as if this chastisement were a command performance put on expressly for their benefit.

'Frantzin set me on my feet, adjusted my skirt, and he was so handsome, nostrils quivering like when he tamed the bolting horses.

' "So little lady," he said, "we're turning over a new leaf."

'He bent down, picked up the No. 3 drafting pen, screwed

the rubber hose back into the pump, and snapped the pump back into the fork on the frame.

'I grabbed the pump, raised it for the bicyclists to see, and spoke thus: "I bought this bicycle pump at Runkas and Company on Boleslavi Street." '

'Runkas and Company on Boleslavi Street,' mumbled a rapt Blaise. Angels are forbidden to peep; that is, to read people's thoughts, for instance, or spy on bathing women, men, children, and prairie wolves – unless of course it happens to be part of their duties on the job, but Blaise, a most disciplined angel for a novice, was so astounded by Cho-Cho's comment (worthy of the angel Murmur) on Anna's behind (it was almost as if he had heard his own thought spoken), that, blushing, he sought sanctuary in Anna's thoughts. However, Anna being a creature of uninhibited tongue and a sensual one, the angel got more out of his new refuge than he had bargained for.

He was very much taken with this woman. He looked with reverence at Cho-Cho, who, impassive, sat beside him in the car. Will he ever achieve this state of equanimity, his soul fully satisfied in the service of the Lord, instead of hankering, like now, for Anna's curvaceous behind? He was blissfully unaware of the shiver that engulfed Cho-Cho, waves of hot and cold, whenever he thought of Blaise, his young colleague.

Commie blues, *proletkult* blues, *Staatssicherheits* blues, secret police ÁVÓ blues, reform blues, *perestroika* blues, dollar blues, this is what Blaise scanned in Anna's brain, who, however, was whistling the 'Worthless Woman Blues' – Roy Orbison, the angel knew. And now he committed the other transgression *vis à vis* peeping, that of peeping into the future.

'Listen, Cho-Cho, old pal, better tell your junior partner there to get in tune with the collective, *in concerto* with the divine order of things, if you get my drift, once we've chewed it over and cut the deal, then that's that . . . No call for solo improvisation, freelance shitting in your pants, no need to be quite so *Hungarian*, lay the coordinates on him again, will ya, there's a good boy, Cho-Cho, heavenly messenger of mine . . . And let's roll it on one take, all right already?!'

The Good Lord liked order; I could refer here to Tolstoy, for instance, he'd get real annoyed at this sort of runaround. To be conscious of everyone's consciousness, giving free rein yet bearing the brunt of the responsibility – well then, the plot should proceed according to plan, at least, in good order . . . Obviously, the Lord had not thought this thing through all the way! (Though to give him his due, he was in a tight spot.)

From that infinitesimal shiver which ran like a breeze through Anna as she stretched, Blaise could see the Anna of the future, lying in bed, first her head would start to ache, her body growing hot, while a cold sweat like a hateful, alien piece of clothing, would slither up and down her back and temples, then she would start shivering, a growing tremor shaking her whole body, as if an engine (a Lada 1600 engine) were rattling inside her to no purpose, idling; the children would call the writer, come quick, there's something wrong, and Blaise could see what Anna would also see an hour later, the sulky expression on the writer's face, 'it's always the same expression when I'm sick, when there's some *problem* with me, if he only had the nerve, he'd shrink with disgust.'

Anna would be trembling so hard, so helplessly, that the writer would have to hold her down, with a gesture that's like an embrace. Teeth chattering, biting the words in half, biting the words out of the dark, through this chattering of her teeth Anna would say: 'I think I am with child.'

'You mean pregnant?' the writer would ask oafishly.

'Yes.'

'That's great,' this from the writer, as above.

At this, Anna's hysterical scream would rise, barely more than a hiccup, what's great?! what?! at which the writer would start stroking her hair, at which Anna would tell him to fuck off, howling that nobody had better touch her. The children would be frightened, and also angry. The screaming would scare the writer, too; what really happened would slowly dawn on him at last . . . 'It's out of the question, Bohumil, that you, for instance, could be such a jerk . . .', at which Anna would break into sobs, and in the end it would be this, and not the embrace, but this other quaking that would subdue this inexorable something.

Blaise was not prepared for this sudden silence. Besides, he got the chronology all muddled up, and he panicked.

'Go!' he screamed at the dozing Cho-Cho, who, still half asleep, turned on the ignition, just like he was taught at the police academy, the tires screeched, and only after taking a right, safely out of firing range, did he open his eyes to give his partner a look of gentle reproach.

Bit by bit, Anna's tears dried up; she sniffled, cleared her throat, blew her nose. The writer was sitting on the edge of the bed, bent and stooped like an old man, arms dangling between his legs, his glasses slid down to the tip of his nose, his hair falling straight, like a threadbare curtain, over one side of his face. No, not even an old man, more like an old woman.

A Lada engine was started up outside. Anna sat up and listened. As if she had forgotten about crying, she said that she had seen two men in front of the house. In a car. The writer did not stir. And that they drove off in a most *peculiar* manner.

'What do you mean, peculiar?' the writer asked mechanically. He did not have to listen to the sense of a sentence, he did not have to understand a sentence to know when something was amiss. That they drove off just when she, Anna, went out to the garden.

'A car like that always drives off "just when",' the writer said testily. Without meaning to, both became suddenly very sober and practical. But the neighbours say those two had been cruising around here before. Were they snooping? Yes, they were snooping. But this is Eastern-European paranoia. Eastern-European paranoia is the fear of being snooped on when you are being snooped on.

'But we're not being snooped on unless you take into account that everybody is being snooped on – provided that they are.' Still, the writer should go outside and check. He shrugged, went outside, came back; there was nothing out there. Anna jumped off the bed, lost her balance, grabbed the clothes-tree, which came tumbling down, then continued running, through the children's room.

'What do you mean nothing? You call that nothing? They're out there, I can hear them!' As soon as she reached the window she saw them there, across the streeet, beyond the telephone pole, two men sitting motionless in the car, looking up, here, at her, at the window; see, there they are, and always were – but then the younger of the two, a man with a black stubble, raised an ethereal pale hand with a tired fanning motion, as if he meant to wave, then he let three fingers drop, only the index finger still stayed pointing up as it fluttered in warning to his lips, gently prodding Anna to silence.

Anna blushed, and, she had no idea why, unexpectedly and inexplicably turned back from the window without a word. They were all looking at her, the three children and the one man. She shrugged. In the mirror she did not want to see that dishevelled, overworked woman with circles under her eyes, a face puffy from tears, who, putting her hand on her belly, kept repeating with downturned mouth, over and over again, like one rehearsing: – No, no, no, no . . .

26

6

There is such a thing as emptiness. The next morning was empty, no car of any kind outside, the writer absorbed in his work. 'See, Bohumil, my love, here we are, just the two of us. This little pig went to market, this little pig stayed at home, this little pig had a bit of meat, and this little pig had . . .'

Anna loved to talk.

'I'm going to make chicken soup. I'm going to try out the idea of "soup as a one-dish meal" on my family. And watch them gripe. And smack their lips. Cooking I learned from my husband's mother. I'm ungrateful, but I speak the truth: from my own mother I learned nothing. I could have learned fear from her, like from my father and older brother; fear of the system, of one's workplace, fear of everything unknown, fear of life, of God, of the foul fiend, fear of each other, of myself, fear of fear itself. Actually, I wouldn't have even known what fear was like, I would have been so deeply immersed in it. I could have learned all this, but I did not. From my quiet and gentle and intimidated mother I could also have learned quiet and gentleness . . .'

'Fate' brought her mother-in-law (of the future) and herself 'together' in January of 1970; she was nineteen at the time, and taken to distraction with this woman's son, and he with her. When she was dragged out to the house where they now lived and was introduced, Anna – woman to woman – could see that the boy's mother had *made preparations*, her lips were freshly rouged, and when she later saw in the bathroom that only the ceiling light was working, the one above the mirror having burnt out, she understood what had frightened her a little at first: why the powder was heaped up on the woman's face, exaggerated, grotesque, piles of cement on a neutral terrain.

'You could tell that my husband's father, he's not easily *budged*, what I mean is, he had been ordered to attend, like me, he had been driven there, rounded up, in short, that this was a reception in earnest. The formal mode of address, no first names, was what he had decided on. We eventually switched to a first-name basis after my second child was born. Or was it because it was a boy? That I was able to present their son with a son? To carry on the family name? There's so much to *fret* about in a well-defined family such as my husband's . . . Tell me, old friend, what will happen if there is no one to carry on my name? . . . Of course, if the name is small enough, it doesn't have to be carried, it can carry itself . . . Thus do small and great merge . . .

Though I could be wrong. And it's the 'small' that thinks this way about the 'great'. That maybe these people want to live forever, and that's why they don't forget, that's why they refuse to forget . . . So it's not just by living on in their kids . . . they've got something else in mind as well . . . others . . . it is time itself that lives on in them! Time accrues to them, the time of their grandfathers, the time of their grandfathers' grandfathers, historical time, the nation's time . . . But this, too, might be an exaggeration. In any case, on this kind of family occasion, the way my father-in-law and my husband and his brothers carry themselves, though they may be bored and indifferent, you can see this ponderous *clannishness* on them. Whether they know it or not, whether they want it or not, whether for better or for worse.'

'Still, all of you put together, objectively speaking, are no deb's delight,' Anna remarked years later, by way of summing up her experiences. For, like it or not, it followed from this clannishness that there came to be strangers in the family. The wives, and no one dared or wanted to say this in so many words, were strangers. 'In a *certain sense*, these people regarded even their own mothers as strangers.' The monsters. The monsters were largely ignorant of all this; it wasn't they who suffered. Among the strangers there were some who were restless, some who were intimidated, some who were calm and grateful, but they all sought, deliberately, or with a vengeance, a chance to work some of it off, no matter how little. Forces that make a family endure, and a family-wrecking cruelty, all rolled into one.

'You're harbouring vipers in your bosoms.'

'It's not bosoms,' said the writer tersely. (Having 'deserted to Haydn's side', he was also a wife himself, in a way.)

'Still, it's a godsend that you're no longer the ruling class.'

'A godsend. For everyone concerned.' It was at this point that Anna let drop the remark about the writer's family, objectively speaking, being no deb's delight.

'Oh, sure, objectively speaking,' said the writer pompously as he was getting undressed, an indirect Amoroso, a resistible male.

'Still, I like to imagine the scene, a hundred years ago, let's say, as I tell my father-in-law, the ice-cold, albeit enlightened, despot: Our Father. My child, whom I have just brought into the world, your grandson . . . I have decided, and my decision is final . . . will bear the illustrious name of *Hrabal*. Oh, they'd disown me without a second thought. They wouldn't even ask what a hrabal was. As a matter of principle. That's what makes an aristocratic family like this so loveable, the way they *protect* themselves. From themselves. With my lord and master, the progeny, a true Hrabal, in arm, off we'd march, with the estate behind, poor as paupers. We'd settle down in Prague, which consequently we'd despise, just a little. Only my mother-in-law's clandestine, monthly pecuniary remissions would serve as a reminder of the luxurious life that I would have left behind because of you, Bohush, sweets.

'When I was left alone with my father-in-law for the first time in my life, I looked at him, grinned, and proceeded to sing for him the "Tax-Free Blues".

Sweet man / why bother? / what's the use? /
I love you / don't bother / forget it /
just love me too / and forget it /
and don't file / that nasty /
tax return / it's dawning / so don't.

'We eyed each other. He raised his eyebrows. I shrugged apologetically.

' "Save that for my son," he said with some annoyance, and patted my cute little cheeks. He was right not to take me seriously. – "By the way, may I point out that there is a certain tendency in modern economics to distinguish between taxes and customs duty," he added so . . . not exactly sweetly, but warbling, as if he did take me seriously after all.'

Anna was enchanted by her father-in-law; that forehead, those glasses, the haughty, or rather, proud and humble, i.e., ironic eyes which she has since come to know so well from another face, related to his; the laughter, meant for himself, really, bursting forth unexpectedly and trailing off unexpectedly, his playful manner of speaking, his cleverness, what a merciless intellect!, the greying hair (or the other way around, as if some dark had mingled in among the white), the squinting cobwebs in the corner of his eye, his hand, looking so heavy and so strong, his schoolboyish leanness, the resemblance between himself and his son, which could not be tied to any one particular detail of the body and therefore seemed even more essential and significant; maybe it was the pauses, the way they fell silent and watched, probing, not the effect, more than the effect, the consequences ('was there blood drawn, and whose?'); this silence of theirs was tellingly similar – silence as part of the body; a spellbounding man, was all Anna could think of at first. (Later she thought of other things besides.)

Darkness falls early in January, but it was still light outside; nevertheless, the dark brown drapes were drawn together. Her mother-in-law did not like sunlight, she seemed to have it in for the sun, Anna never found out why. (Maybe it was her headaches. She used to suffer from migraine for weeks on end, though this was barely noticed by her family; she merely lost her smile, a spasm set on her face, like a veil or a furry coating, or rather a lifelessness, with sharper shadows, but she still saw to all the housework; the family had to cut down on the noise, but that was all. The writer is the heir. 'These people always have an heir . . .') Dark brown drapes, shiny, dark green upholstery, elegant yellow lampshades of silk, the brown, the green, the yellow – these colours became engrained into both of them, into Anna and the writer; it was amusing to see, they found it amusing, how in their later homes they unconsciously sought these colours, how they always ended up with these colours.

In the course of the long afternoon coffee, people gradually paired off, pairs were formed, short-lived, unreliable unions which didn't really have any aim anyway, unless it was the self-justification that pairs could actually exist. Anna was taken by surprise, the pairs were so quick to change, independent of their success (the two women were the most effective by a long shot, and the most awkward, as was only to be expected, the young couple); it wasn't the game itself that surprised her, nor the fact that there was in this give-and-take something that was less than shameless, or more impersonal: a touch of frivolity (as much – Anna did not know this at the time, she found this out by the writer's side – as in any game;

the seriousness of playing is one thing, and the seriousness outside the game something else again), but that all this should be orchestrated by two serious-minded adults – because her mother-in-law seemed very stern and serious, indeed, and even her father-in-law's inattentiveness carried a strain of warning – this is what surprised her, this *grown-up messiness*. At her parents', everything was always in perfect order.

She wore that light green dress of hers that she made herself, as a consequence of which the material was bunched up at one shoulder, making tiny ripples, inadvertent frills, and in this constant and therefore irritated tugging her bra strap showed (at the collar bone.) 'That little green thing you whipped up yourself,' is how the writer used to refer to it, provided he referred to it at all. One might think that the dress was awry on one side because her breasts were awry. That one might be bigger than the other. But they were identical. 'I look at my daughters to see which one inherited my body. I have two bodies, one a thinner, more muscular, wiry body (the *infinite* girl's), the body before my marriage, and I have a more rounded, softer body (the *eight* girl's), one of these went to my older, the other to my younger daughter; and by now there is a third body as well, this tormented one, the body worn down by children and the passing of time, this is a heavier and more sluggish body, but we get on, I'd like to force it this way and that, to convince it, basically, to keep itself in shape, be less, but it won't listen, well then, don't!

'Wailing, the smallest one ran out of the bathroom the other day, everybody rushed over, "Oh! oh! it just caved in!" she sobbed. "What caved in, and where?" her father asked anxiously, probably thinking of the chores around the house. The little one broke into a grin, "It just caved in, the water just caved in under mummy!" There they stood in the bathroom door, my very own kith and kin, with that identical grin on their faces, like quadruplets. And they nodded, were in profound agreement, yes, siree, why beat about the bush, the water under *momma* had caved in, truly it had. As if they had felt sorry for the water. For a while I laughed along with them, but then I stopped laughing.'

'Let's leave the men to fend for themselves,' the writer's mother said, and they went out to the kitchen. She watched the girl put on a fresh pot of coffee and wash two plates as a matter of course. This put her mind at ease. She recognized herself in this skinny newcomer (the stranger who appears in this great big family, and doesn't even know that though she is not necessarily expected to be frightened, she should at least have the good sense to look awed), and therefore dealt cautiously with her at first. Brusquely, rather than stand-offishly. On the other hand, she took an immediately liking to the girl. She played the grand heroic scene of 'the mother's first dramatic confrontation with her son's seductress' well, with determination and to the letter, but soon grew tired of it, laughed, shrugged, and then Anna saw that it would be all right like this – the two of them together.

She stroked Anna's cheek. Her hand was velvety, light, and smelled nice. And it was red and scaly.

'Yours will be like that too!' she said softly as she studied the girl's face.

She had suspected that Anna was her son's sweetheart. The thing must have happened on Wednesday and Friday mornings – when the *two of them* happened, in line with the writer's college schedule. It surprised him, too, that his mother played along without asking any questions or raising any difficulties. Because of Anna's impatience, more than once they almost ran into each other in front of the house, had the woman not studied with such absorption the truly not uninteresting crests of the poplars across the street, or the fascinating emptiness of the deserted public beach. She always got dressed up on these mornings (thus becoming an accessory? but no, that's going too far); she looked especially fetching in a soft, yellow suit with fist-size blue buttons, sent from Milan by her sister-in-law, whom she heartily detested. Following the classical pattern, she went to the movies. For some reason, she'd see nothing but Hungarian films; she became terrifically well versed in the new wave: Kósa's *Judgement*, Gaál's *The Green Years*, Szabó's *Love Film*, Makk's *Love*; this latter was her favourite, along with Jancsó.

'Once in a while she grumbled, why must she stay away the entire morning? Well, how many minutes did you have in mind, mother?'According to my husband, my mother-in-law *nearly* told him. This, too, forged a bond between us, this coming and going. We preferred to share her son rather than fight over him.

'She loved me as a daughter – she only had sons – but she put one over on me when it came to the automatic washing machine. They bought everything (it never even occurred to them that this might embarrass us), quickly, she bought us a small East German machine, and *on the side*, a centrifuge wringer. I wonder why. With four children of her own, she must have known what washing entailed.

'I catch my pet-with-a-mother-complex studying my hand on the sly, looking for his mother's, unable to find it; by now, oh hand cream of hand creams, almighty *Fulcinar*! my own hands are thoroughly devastated, too, though not quite in the same way – sorry, old boy! . . .

'Did my mother-in-law want me to find out what it was like, working? But why? She knew, she knew perfectly well, she knew even better than that, that I'd find out, I'd work my fingers to the bone by her darling son's side, and her darling son's sons' side, so what did she have in mind? And I know that she knew. Use it in good health, dear, she said nodding absentmindedly. There are all sorts of names for this, but the best is cruelty. *That I shouldn't have it any better than she did.*

'I exchanged it the same day. (For the type she had, a good automatic.) She didn't say a word; nonchalantly, without real anger, she gave me the eye. – Poor thing, if she had only known that with the third child I'd have it so darned good, I'd go and prefer (I'd actually *plan ahead* to prefer) disposable diapers from Vienna over the antiquated cotton ones . . . And do you know why, Bohumil? Because I hate diapers. And do you know why? Because they stink. So now you know. Incidentally, the timing with which your colleague avoids the vicinity of the diapers is worthy of a candidate for political office. I mean, it's world-class. And the crying, how there's no such thing, crying babies are a matter of definition; after all, who'd have the presumption to differentiate between a light crowing and a soft sob, not to mention a squeal of sheer contentment! Besides, there's a way to quiet down a bawling child. And what might that be? The door, he giggles, shut the door; besides, our progeny are *just the type* to cry themselves to sleep, he'd tried it out a thousand times before, and truly, my poor little orphans, up to their ears in shit, screaming their heads off behind distant, closed doors, this is their offering on the altar of literature, *non olet.*'

'Aha. So that's what you're like,' the writer's mother must have thought. 'Fine. You'll need all that stubbornness.' Later, she told Anna a lot of things; she told her about her own life, about how difficult it is among so many men. She complained proudly. Difficult, this word kept recurring; she even told her things she had never told her son. These Anna passed on to the writer with just a little (a very little) twinge of bad conscience.

'My in-laws moved here in the spring of '57, after the

previous tenant had defected . . . You know, there's that joke about staying at home out of a sense of adventure . . . Bohumil! This family of my husband's, they were very rich before the war, *filthy* rich, like that Doctor Guntorad and the board of managers of the brewery all rolled into one, let's say, and even richer than that, so you can imagine.' Sometimes Anna would cast clandestine glances at her father-in-law, trying to imagine him as a prince – indeed, he had actually been brought up to be something of the kind, raised to rule over a territory, over people, educated to be their *owner*; she tried to coax out the prince from her father-in-law's countenance, but saw only an attractive silvery man, an engaging, taciturn father.

In June 1951, the authorities forced the family to leave Budapest and resettle in a village.

Anna kept a photograph taken in 1952; her mother-in-law had put it in her hand once.

'Hang on to this, dear,' she said.

The picture shows three peasants standing in the field, their arms weighted down by centuries of toil, their sunburnt, rough necks partly covered by their buttoned-up shirts. There is no difference between them, their fathers must have looked just like this, and their fathers' fathers before them. One of them, ever so slightly, looks as if he were a little more bent than the other two. He is smiling for the camera, a dull dread in his eyes. His forehead, which is *higher* than the usual, glistens with sweat. He is thirty-three years old. He is at rock bottom – despoiled, dispossessed, though otherwise in the prime of life, as they say. He has nothing except his family, and that, too, what for? He reads, writes, and speaks three languages (how lucky can you get?), a doctor of law and political science – the prince. When at the close of the scorching summer's day he'll trample home in the heavy night, covered with dust, his son will be waiting for him at the gate, a whining two-year-old towhead whose name, for Anna, is the most precious among all men's names.

When Stalin died, the gates to the internment camps were flung open ('these were not death camps, after all, there were no SS soldiers there, only ÁVÓ soldiers who beat people up, and withheld their food, but you can't compare that to a Buchenwald or Bergen-Belsen, now can you? They beat people up, innocent people, while in Buchenwald they shot innocent people and sent them, innocent, to the gas chambers; I wouldn't even call it an internment camp, I don't know what I should call it; here, at least if you fell ill, you were taken to the infirmary, under the care of Doctor Ács, who said, you have to go to the mines because, as far as that goes, it's red, all right, but it's not that swollen, or else that it's swollen, all right, but it's not that red, off to the mines, you hear?! and when you were in a really bad state, swollen as can be and red as can be, you could lie in at the infirmary, on a bag of straw on the floor'), the guards patted the inmates on the back, 'See you around, old man, we made it after all,' as if nothing had happened; they were even made to sign a piece of paper to that effect, that nothing happened to them, and the officially appointed punitive quarters and relocations were also discontinued.

But those who had been relocated were slow to win forgiveness for having suffered this injustice, and though they were no longer scoundrels, just second-class citizens, they were not allowed to come straight back to Budapest, and generally chose to settle in the villages and small towns around the capital, such as Pomáz or Érd. 'My husband tells me that when in May '54 they entered that always dark basement apartment in Csobánka where they had to keep a washbowl by the wall, by evening it would fill with water to the brim – for some reason, he is very proud of this, the fact that the washbowl always *got filled* to the brim; maybe for him this illustrates the degree of their privations – my mother-in-law was waiting for them, she was the same age as I am now, and the two children were holding their father's hand, and the room was crowded with toys, what I mean is, there was a rubber ball with polka dots, and there was a train strung together out of empty (yellow, Danish!) sardine cans (when pulled along in the sawdust, it automatically created its own rails, real neat!); because of all this, and the holiday expressions on the two adults' faces, they thought it was Christmas. They weren't bothered by the warm weather, but where was the tree, the Christmas tree? my mother-in-law had hung the fresh wash on the fir outside the house, the coloured shirts, the underwear, red, blue, yellow, white, there it was, the Christmas tree, see, right there! . . .'

For a long time, the writer and his brothers used the formal mode of address with their parents.

'Mother, please, would you kindly tell little Jesus that he could have brought that Christmas tree inside.' – But it's so nice and big. That's true. Still, why didn't little Jesus think *ahead*? But they've never had a Christmas tree quite so big before. Still, he can't understand this *reluctance* on Jesus's part. At which the writer's father slammed his fist on the table so hard that the glasses and cutlery trembled for some time. He had turned thirty-five on that day; in the middle of his journey through life, he had entered a thick, dark forest.

7

Young Blaise was not fully cognizant of the sociological and historical repercussions of the earthly guises they had chosen to adopt; he did not realize that the policeman, the secret police officer from the ÁVÓ, the soldier, the fireman – uniforms in general – as far as the man on the street was concerned, all authority (as such) was one and the same; in any case, I don't buy the extremist Gnostic tradition which regards all material forms as the cloak of Lucifer; so then, the angel did not realize – oh, those details! those details! – that 'when the medical corps sergeant removed the dressing, the hand was already putrefied, and the stench so overwhelming that the major got sick'; he did not realize that 'the doctor at the secret police, when he threw the amputated hand in the bucket, said, "You'll never play the piano again",' which prediction had doubtless held true to this day, to be sure; he did not realize that in the back of the car, 'under the dirty linen, there lay the corpse of the captain, a military court judge'; he did not realize that in '48, for instance, the commissariat for finance still had scruples, because if they took someone's father and uncle in, for instance, and beat one of them to death, for instance, they'd let the other go; he did not realize that if beaten enough, just about anyone will sign just about anything – if after the soles of his feet are beaten to a pulp, and he is then made to walk on gravel with his bloody stumps, pieces of flesh hanging loose, if his kidneys are kicked until they are ruptured, if hobnailed boots stomp on his back and chest until every one of his ribs is crushed (so that even today, every breath brings a grimace to his face, and each sigh a strange look in his eyes), if they pierce his eardrums, if they flick a cigarette lighter on very close to his eyes with quick jerks of the thumb (this works even better, the effect is further enhanced, if done by a triumphantly beautiful eighteen-year-old girl), if his nails are torn out, if a little milkie is injected into his lungs, or high voltage shot up his prick; he did not realize that they forced drops of water up the victim's nose, which made the man scream and choke, not because they were cruel or biased, but because it is practical, it leaves no trace, there is no blood, no fractures, haematomas, puss, inflamed wounds, swollen joints, torn tendons, knocked-out teeth, splintered bones; he did not realize that wrapping someone in a wet sheet until it dries is not a sadistic, perverse, Bolshevik invention, but a technique deeply rooted in the traditions of all hunting, fishing, trapping tribes: the drying animal skin was a sure-fire method of strangulation; and although the angel understood that crowds had been fired upon, he did not understand that the next day the entire square had to be repaved, because they could not scrub all the blood off in one night (yes, indeed, this they had not counted on!); he understood that crowds had been fired upon, but not that they were also shot at from above, from aeroplanes, like at a hunt; he understood that crowds had been fired upon, but not that thirty-three years later, though with the faintest trace of a stammer, they'd categorically deny it (+ a pension); he understood that they pardoned people, but not that the pardon was read out under the gallows; he understood that a man was shovelled under in the prison yard, at night, like a thief, an awkward case, but not that they piled the place full of furniture, so they wouldn't even have to look at it; he understood that the man had been scraped under, like a dog, but not that this happened in a bone yard, among the bones of giraffes, elephants, lynxes and jackals, wrapped in paper and bound with wire, face down into the soil, at times in pairs, the protruding, stately extremities bent back, this he did not know; all that the angel waiting in the Lada knew or felt was what was radiating toward him from the neighbourhood, the houses, the windows, the chimneys, from the way people averted their heads and quickened their pace, the way their eyelashes fluttered – that this, this was not love.

Cho-Cho studied the elegant, elongated oval of young Blaise's face, the dark moonglow of his complexion under the stubble.

'Don't take it to heart, my angel. Nowhere on earth are nations guided by love. Just look around you from New York to Peking, from Stockholm to Sidney, from Békéscsaba to Gyula. Maybe the law. Or maybe not even the law, just the memory of the law. The jerking spider's leg that is the memory of the spider. A shadow-world.'

'A vale of tears.'

'I don't know about that. No need to go overboard, old pal . . . Stars, now stars are guided by love, all of them.' Cho-Cho knew that the other was frightened, and so he stroked the coal-black mop of his partner's head.

'How could the Good Lord allow this thing?! How?' Little Blaise moaned. The ruby light of the stick shift was more like a shriek.

'How, how, and the cat's miaow, that's how! Besides, it's been elucidated, theologically speaking. And I'm no first prize at the heavenly sweepstakes myself. Can't even prevent a piddling abortion. Or can I?!'

It was at this juncture that Anna came through the garden gate. Was she going shopping or to the doctor? The older man nudged the younger out of the car.

'Snap out of it, and go after her,' he hissed. He was not jealous. On the contrary. 'Time does not exist,' he added in a whisper, 'only feelings,' and he winked in complicity. 'Only what is real is true.' Blaise flinched.

'Oh, but that would be awful!' None the less, mesmerized by the woman, the next instant he was shadowing her like a sleepwalker. She pretended not to notice him.

'Look here, Angelus. This is no time for a heart-to-heart with your little buddy, dig? . . . I can't be present at every sexual turn-on. I haven't got the time!' Hearing the word time, the angel started to giggle. 'What the two of you are doing is terrible, it's *schrecklich.*' Nobody spoke. The Lord sighed wearily. 'So then, what now?' Hardly a question, a statement, rather, a serious statement, so then, what now?

'Lord, you are jealous of Blaise.'

'Look who is calling the kettle black.'

'Excuse me?'

'Forget it. Over and out.'

Hosanna to you, Intellect! (Forehead to the ground. Intermission.)

8

'Soup is not *really* my forte. As I see it, soup takes patience plus raw materials, while I'm short on patience, and can't stand going to the market. The moment of truth, that's chicken soup, you can't cheat on chicken soup. An onion soup or a cream of celery soup, that's a matter of dexterity. Or sleight-of-hand, if you will. I think as a housekeeper I am both very good and very bad. And above all, I am not reliable.

'On the other hand, I have no equal in preparing meat, especially beef and veal – specifically, the rump steak we all pretend is tenderloin. Or if I do, it makes no difference . . . Although I grant you that a good rump steak is also a matter of grace. (Not as much as meat in aspic, though; you should ask my husband about that – Bohumil, you'd never believe this, but my husband can actually make meat in aspic; real, down-to-earth, honest-to-goodness meat in aspic, none of your fancy *haute cuisine* mish-mosh . . . He says it can't be learned, you've got to know everything, put everything into it, then *wait* . . .)

'The best steak of my life I made for a stranger. Not a complete stranger, but the mailman, an unhappy mailman. He happened to be most unhappy when I opened the door for him. You're a real pro at that, Bohumil, about a door opening, and someone standing there, unhappy. You must have watched closely. Well, so have I . . . I'm going to cook for you one day. Sauerbraten in brown sauce. And I wouldn't shrink from attempting the semolina dumplings either. Dumplings for a native Czech! Why settle for less, my dear, don't you agree? There the two of you would be, you and my husband, in the kitchen, leaning on your elbows, munching, need I say it? munching and smacking your lips, and I'd watch you eat. Of course, there'd be plums, too, don't worry. And the two of you wouldn't say a word, none of that disgusting father-son literary soul-to-soul stuff, you'd just eat, shovel it in, and from time to time you'd give each other a look, then me, then the dumplings. Naturally, you'd be drinking beer, it's good for springtime fatigue, Gosslar'sche Gosse, of course. That's how I imagine it.

'When the doorbell rang I opened the door, and right away the mailman started weeping, sniffling, sniffling, tears streaming down his cheeks; and because he tried to hold it back, in his embarrassment he produced a thin, sing-song little whine, as if the sound was being squeezed through a crack. He was around forty, the age we are now.'

This happened ten years ago. Anna liked that small apartment where they started their life together, those forty-eight square metres, which through all those years they thought were fifty-two, because they had bought it as fifty-two, until it was time to sell, that's when they became forty-eight – a number from which, to resort to cliché, they refused to budge. Even with two children it did not seem cramped – nor ideal, for that matter; to get work done, the writer would

43

escape here and there, to libraries, but chiefly into the night, because he liked being at home and working there, he liked it when everyone was at home and it was dead still, 'that subtle intake of breath as they sleep, that I like,' he'd spout off, and shifted his working hours to the night, got up at noon, puttered about till the evening, waiting for everyone to fall asleep.

'Do you love me.'

'Sure. Just go to sleep.'

Portrait of a man in love (with ermine), second half of the 1970s . . . One might think that the tiny apartment was not cramped because Anna and the writer got on so well, nearly without bitterness, in fact, and had great hopes; when Anna thought back to those times now, she saw the two of them at thirty, so confident, so calm, a pleasant feeling; full of plans, working like the dickens, every day bright in its own light, lots of people coming over, not the 'in crowd', but true friends, someone showing up almost every day, part-strangers 'dropping by', and somehow, everyone expected something of everyone else, something good, that the other one would also accomplish something good in the world; Anna cooked delicious meals, young men and women sashayed greeting each other in the summer night. They could just about feel their lives taking off, and they were jubilant.

'In short, the apartment was a home, and this home roomy, that's how we liked to think of it. It definitely helps to have a so-called "picture" window, an entire wall made of glass, so to say; opening the box circumscribed by the walls into the infinite, it expands toward the sky, there is no end to it, and whoever is sitting inside becomes a tenant of the cosmos, and this way, the crescent moon and the pile of books waiting to be shelved become companions of equal rank *inside* the apartment. Whoever visited us at the time must have felt this potential, this unexpected spaciousness.

'I can just hear you, Bohush love, mumbling something about how that poor mailman couldn't help but cry when he entered this holy of holies: infinitude, stars, love, friendship, a future, find me one mailman, honey, who wouldn't break into . . .

'But that's not why he was weeping. There was a woman, naturally. He handed me my letters, and just stood there, sniffling quietly. I made him sit down in the kitchen. I had gotten hold of some rump steak a few days before and had put it in oil and onions to marinate. Then we found people for the steak. We were expecting them for dinner.

'The mailman started up again, sobbing his heart out, no kidding, he was beginning to scare me; let me tell you, this male sobbing can be very unnerving, I remember my father back in '56 . . . He looked at me as if I was supposed to know something, I mean, as if I was supposed to absolve him, because he, so the mailman said, had cheated on his wife, and now he's happy, but his wife is trying, in cahoots with of all people his own mother, to take his happiness away, they want to steal his happiness, snatch it away from him, and after all, they're right, a child's no joking matter, that's why he's unhappy, because his happiness is illicit, on the other hand, now, with this girl, he knows that he's at last what he should be, he's what he'd imagined himself to be like, she's a young girl from the office, fresh as a daisy, just what the doctor ordered, who can read his eyes, he'd never known love could be this playful, that, for instance, he smooths down his hair and *she's the only one to notice*, this other one, and he can't go on living a lie any more, it's hell, his wife, by the way, has a college education, while he's just a mailman, not that this has ever been a source of conflict between them, on the other hand, he did study theology in night school, and then once, when he thanked his wife for folding his shirts, his wife, a

45

construction engineer, not an architect, a builder, it's not the same! his wife said, laughing, laughing like in the movies, that if my husband thanks me for folding his shirts, then my husband must have a lover. To which he said yes.

'You can imagine, Bohumil, where I was by then! The meat had matured nicely; I could feel it the moment I took it out, from its touch and handle, the way it behaved under my fingers. I placed it in very hot oil, under a lid, for a short spell, it never hurts, with beef, this steaming, I had some pickled tarragon left, so I sprinkled that on, on an impulse, you know how I am! opened a bottle of burgundy, shoved the mailman's bag aside with my foot, and served. He asked no questions, but picked up his knife and fork, I had to shout at him to wait for me. Then I remembered the green peas and mushrooms, and spooned some on top of each steak. Bohumil: this was in the early autumn of 1979, and I haven't made such a tender and rare, butter-soft, and well-seasoned rump steak since . . .

'Enter my husband – your colleague – by which aside I do not mean to shift any of the blame on you. By then we were into the second bottle of wine, and I had taken the poor thing out to the loggia for some fresh air, so he shouldn't sit so pale in that dark kitchen.'

The writer tried to guess who the stranger was. The bag gave him the clue.

'And imagine,' said Anna, pointing to the mailman, 'sometimes at night he'd just sit in the dark, looking around in his own apartment as if he didn't belong there.' The writer nodded; he understood as much as he could. He wasn't feeling well. After a while he asked, what about the letters? What letters? The letters that were suppposed to be delivered. There's just this street left to go. He went back to the kitchen and took the letters – the mail – out of the huge bag (it's the first time he'd ever been into a mailman's bag). Outside, Anna began to whistle Sonny Boy's 'Little John'.

Little John, / Ask your daddy / Daddy, does the Lord / See in the dark? / In the dark the Lord / Sees nothing, / Little John, / Only daddy / Only daddy / Sees in the dark, / Little John.

He looked at the table with its remnants, worried about the leftovers. Anna and the mailman he saw as if they were sitting behind a curtain: Anna was whistling and humming, the mailman murmuring the lyrics and swaying his head to the rhythm.

He went and delivered the mail, dropped the postcards, letters and occasional newspapers into mailboxes. The small street wound its way up to the top of the hill in a fine, sweeping spiral like a peeled apple skin. At the top, the writer stopped and looked back. The lights were already on in the valley. 'In the dark the Lord sees nothing, only daddy, only daddy sees in the dark,' he muttered. He thought of his father. He did not attach any symbolic significance to delivering the mail ('getting the message across', 'service'); he just felt good because he had finished a task. What one of them had begun, another had finished. When he got back, Anna was alone, doing the dishes. He smiled.

'I even got a tip.'

'You just want to appear better than you are, playing the mailman . . .'

'No doubt. On the other hand, I see in the dark. *Darkness, darkling*' . . .

Each was in high spirits, each for a different reason. But Anna avoided looking into the writer's eyes. When the guests arrived for the rump steak, a laughing Anna embraced them.

'God, I'm glad you're here . . . Now at last the day can end.'

47

Ever since, there are a number of people in Budapest who have a name for the nonexistent, the almost fulfilled promise, the fantastic possibility that is deception and self-delusion yet fantastic all the same. They call this *Anna's steak à la bonne femme*. And there are two people in Budapest who know that this means something entirely different.

9

(Betrand Russell, patron saint of barbers)
According to military regulations, the army barber can shave only those incapable of shaving themselves, so that, should the barber shave himself, he would then be capable of shaving himself, in which case (in accordance with regulations) he cannot shave himself; he can shave himself only if he cannot shave himself. It is a yes only if it is a no, if it is a no, then it is a yes – a liar will lie, am I lying?

This is the so-called Russell paradox (I beg your pardon, a popularized version thereof), which, according to Sain, embarrassed Frege no end. (*Gottlob* Frege of the lovely name; to which set should be added the Songbird of Prague, Karel Gott. – By the way, without intending to air other people's dirty linen in public, Georg Cantor, the father of the theory of sets, was called by Leopold Kronecker a depraver of youth, and this in public. [Kronecker was Cantor's greatest opponent and former teacher, whose recognition the latter had most wanted to gain.] Cantor, who never doubted the truths he had discovered, was driven to insanity by this lack of appreciation, despite the fact that he had friends who *understood*. While Kronecker, who didn't know the meaning of the word doubt, added, imperturbably as ever: Whole numbers were created by the Good Lord, everything else is man-made. – I think it is the other way around: man forced whole numbers on God; but never mind.)

Frege's book, *Grundgesetze der Arithmetik*, which by this time was at the printer, was shaken to the core by Russell's discovery. The unsuspecting Frege learned about all this from Russell's letter of 16 June 1902. So on 16 June, the mathematicians had to kiss one more of their illusions good-bye; moreover, according to James Joyce, 16 June is the day in which our whole life, indeed existence itself, shines reflected. Anna was born on 16 June, and it was on the same day of the same year that the writer's family was forced to leave their home in Budapest and resettle in a village – they must have reached the compulsory new quarters assigned to them, a *kulák* peasant's house in northern Hungary, just as Anna's mother was getting her one-minute contractions; and it was on this day, seven years later, that Hungary's prime minister was executed, thereby eliminating all obstacles in the way of a new era which, on a strange whim and with a modicum of rationale, was to be called 'the years of consolidation'.

How are we to explain the cutting off of Bohumil Hrabal's mother's hair? With the passage of time? which is as inevitable as the ritual haircutting, the *postriziny*? or that a decision must be made sooner or later? That day was still on the other side of the world war called the first, and which was at least as disappointing, in retrospect, for all mankind, but especially Europe, which as was its wont – and still is – insisted on identifying itself with the whole world (this is what I mean by saying that I am *hopelessly* European), as this Russell affair was for mathematicians. Already at the time of this cutting off of the hair, though independently of it, rescue operations were under way, the logicists, led by Whitehead, were stirring, proceeding from the erroneous premise that mathematics is within the domain of logic, while the intuitionists rallied around Brouwer's banner. Their reliance on inner vision is undoubtedly attractive, yet (in its consequences), to quote once again the excellent Sain (taking the words straight from the horse's mouth), it was very much like trying to stave off illness by resorting to death.

The cutting off of Bohumil Hrabal's mother's hair was the parable of the taming (breaking in) of Bohumil Hrabal's mother, or was it not? Because, if Bohumil Hrabal's mother's hair, as its abundant glory fluttered-cascaded-swept through that idyllic small town, was the symbol of rebellion, then by cutting it off, she indicated that she did not wish to rebel, she wanted to be a good woman. But a good woman does not have her gorgeous, thick mane, admired, revered by the whole town, cut off on a whim. This contradiction Frantzin resolved most elegantly by giving 'the overseer's restless wife' a thorough thrashing on her bum. Put the fear of the Lord in her. Show her who's the master of the house. Except that during this whole scene, Bohumil Hrabal's mother had a good laugh at Bohumil Hrabal's father's expense. But Frantzin was aware of this, that's why he added so quickly, 'as if digging in', OK, little lady, so we're turning over a new leaf. Therefore, his nostrils did not quiver quite as if it were taming the bolting horses, *hola, Ede, Hare, hola istene*! And Bohumil Hrabal's mother – just like the intuitionists, with death as a remedy for illness! – went around this by turning over a new leaf every day? Or if not a new, then an unknown one?

And the fact that she said (admitted, or better yet, *flung in the face* of the bystanders) that she had bought the pump in Boleslavi Street, was that a sign, first and foremost, of some potent inner calm, or could it have meant that her bicycle riding days were over? Or is the idea that it was not a question of *either-or*?

50

Anna would have liked to see clearly in this matter of the hair.

It should be further noted (in connection with Bohumil Hrabal's mother), that the writer also told beautiful and heartfelt stories about his own mother. Please don't think unkindly, he wrote to a distant friend, i.e., to a close friend who happened to be at a distance, and it's no accident this happened when the latter's mother was on her deathbed, don't think unkindly of my mourning, I feel as though everybody were my own mother.

10

'You won't believe this, Bohumil, but when the army of my country marched into your country, my aunt went out of her mind.'

Anna had an aunt, Georgina, her mother's younger sister, fire and water, wolf and lamb (we could go on all day, giving free rein to a trivial dualist reflex: Laurel and Hardy, Goethe and Schiller) – Maria and Georgina. They did not love each other; or to be more exact, Maria did not love Georgina, who in turn simply ignored Maria. Anna was amazed by her mother's vehement and quite open animosity. She did not dare dislike her family; matter-of-factly, she admitted that she had nothing in common with them, neither with her industrious brother, nor with her God-only-knows what kind of father (she couldn't say anything bad about him, or had only bad things to say – in short, nothing), and she had nothing in common with her dead mother either. (Who died in the spring of 1980, growing thinner by the day, a hundred and ten pounds, a hundred, eighty-eight, eighty . . . she wasted away.

Then her mother-in-law, late that summer. Suddenly, they were orphaned, and by definition, grown-ups.)

Thus, without realizing it, Anna came to adopt Georgina's point of view. They saw 'eye to eye' in no time. Her aunt looked remarkably like the ageing Simone Signoret, the same bags under her eyes, *seeing* eyes, an overweight, strong body, sensuous lips, never without rouge, the same hoarse, smoked-out voice – in short, she was the kind of beauty, the kind of feminine beauty, whose every part is ugly, gone bad. For years she'd had difficulty walking, her legs full of water, she had to take diuretics, which wore her out, after a few steps she'd have to stop. 'She would freeze. Like after a pirouette.'

'On 21 August in the summer of '68, Aunt Georgina went out of her mind. Or I don't know. She flipped out. But it was more than that.' At the time she had been drinking a lot, she drank through the summer (drank the summer to *shreds*), got drunk every day, had a way of disappearing, too, forgetting to get off the bus or streetcar, there was the Transportation Authority, going round and round with her, all over town. That day she did not get out of bed; this had happened before, after her 'protracted bouts'; at such times she was cared for by the superintendent, Amata – that was her name, Amata – who brought her bread, bologna and (the first day) beer.

'Take care of yourself, Georgina, dear,' she used to say awkwardly, as if talking to a child. And she was just as nice and helpful even after Georgina had rejected her. On Amata's thirty-fourth birthday they got drunk, shoulder to shoulder, together.

'Let's shack up,' said the thin, brown-skinned woman softly. Georgina kissed her on the lips, laughed, and opened another bottle of beer.

'Forget it, dear. I don't want to live with anyone. It's more than I can handle as is.'

When on that certain 21 August Amata entered the apartment (Georgina never locked the door; at first the superintendent would tactfully lock it from the outside, but there followed a great, drunken tirade: 'anybody that wants to come in does, anyhow; everything's wide open here, everybody's exposed, naked, transparent, the whole country a transit station, and so is every blessed soul in it!'), the foul smell knocked her off her feet, and Georgina, the moment she saw her, broke into tears.

Amata bathed the person so dear to her heart, scrubbed her down and wrapped her in a big, soft, terry-cloth towel, then put clean sheets on the bed. Georgina watched from an easy chair, like a statue, a weeping statue. That same night, the tears were replaced by an apocalyptic fury. She started tugging and shaking Amata, saying that she, she, too, was accountable, no use denying it, she'd better own up, it would all be taken into account by the one created out of fire, out of the breath of the infinite, made in nobody else's image, but aie! enough, for justice would now be dispensed by the fiery sword, no, all would be forgiven – and, with the swiftness of a juggler, she began handing out her blessings and making the sign of the cross.

These attacks eventually got worse, and once, when she tried to strangle Amata, she was taken to the psychiatric ward, but was soon released. At first, Anna could barely recognize her; it wasn't so much her body that had changed, or her face, but the lines of her face, the play of her features. For some months, she became something like a religious fanatic, smiling all the time, receiving Holy Communion every day.

'No confession, though,' she smiled. 'I will not confess to a priest . . .' And with that perpetual smile on her face she added, 'I'm tired, my dear little Anna . . .'

Gradually she regained her former vivacity and stride, the forgotten gestures, drinking less than she used to; on the other hand, it took very little to get her drunk. Anna watched anxiously as she grabbed a glass, with such obvious greed, as if someone were trying to tear it out of her hand. She would visit her aunt now and then, because her aunt wouldn't leave the apartment; this was the change, that ever since that time, she would not leave the apartment. She hadn't left the apartment since 1969.

'She liked my husband.'

'Even those that don't like you like you, isn't that so?' she said to the writer. The writer laughed in embarrassment. Formerly, Anna used to sing the blues for her, but later these sessions faded. Carlsson was Georgina's favourite, little Carlsson, grand-daddy of the Stockholm blues in Stockholm, but it's not so – way before T-Bone Walker sang with the Les Hite Band, shaking his hips in his gold lame suit, anticipating something of Elvis by a good two decades, little Carlsson was already singing and popularizing the 'Breezy Crazy Nose Blood Blues', that brilliant miniature.

> *When your nose is bloody hell*
> *Don't ask where you should dwell*
> *Don't ask what things are worth,*
> *When your nose is bloody and hurt*
> *And your heart's at peace.*

Some Norwegian guy wrote the lyrics.

> *When your heart's about to break, oh,*
> *My sweet guitar, its string goes*
> *(pause): whacko!*

Carlsson's strings also went whacko. When in 1945 he learned about the concentration camps, he wrote a letter to the chief rabbi in Berlin, whose daughter he had met at a concert in Copenhagen, and volunteered for conversion. In his return letter, the chief rabbi politely rejected the idea: 'a Swede is one who thinks of himself as a Swede, but – my dear son – a Jew is one who is singled out as a Jew (and whose mother is a Jew) – Jewish *natus* and not Jewish *doctus*. Believe me, I am not writing this out of pride. It is not easy for me either. Not easy for a Jew, not easy for a would-be Jew. Of Judith, whom you know well, I have no news. She was last seen in Leipzig, among fine, upright people. She is not with us now, but if she were, I know that she would not miss the opportunity to send her warmest regards. If nothing else, the map of Copenhagen she keeps above her bed would surely serve her as a reminder.'

Carlsson never sang again. There was a scandalous radio report once, during the Beatles years, that was aired around the world. A journalist asked Carlsson whether his silence could be construed as a kind of Adorno paraphrase. By then Carlsson was gravely ill, skin cancer or whatever, he had lost weight, he was as tiny and puny as a jockey, and drank a lot. He didn't know Adorno from a paraphase.

'Was it because of Auschwitz that you don't sing, how should I put it, could it be that after Auschwitz it is impossible to sing the blues?' Carlsson tried to clear his throat, hawking up phlegm, you could clearly hear it on the tape. 'Hell, no. I just lost my voice.'

At the time, these two sentences were heard around the world. John Lennon, who loved 'Breezy Crazy', answered every question for an entire week with, 'Hell, no. I just lost my voice.' Anna would have liked to give the same answer many a time but, though Georgina encouraged her, she didn't

55

have the nerve. Lately, they were down to an exchange of letters.

My fragrant little flower, my precious Anna,
I shall show up at your place one fine day – who knows how much longer I can still get around. All the best imaginable for the coming year. And the strength of a Transylvanian bullock, my dove. That's what I used to have myself, I brought it with me from there, but it's ebbing away. Slowly, everything is drying up – I'm losing hair like a mangy cat, even though I am taking precautions. (Everywhere! But let that remain our little secret.) By the way, after all these years, I have reconsidered Amata's offer. Everything is so much calmer this way now.

Hugs and kisses,
Your Aunt Georgina

Anna saw her father cry three times. Once he cried for Georgina, once for the country, and once for himself.

The first time was in 1954, the year that Christmas came to Csobánka in May. Anna and the family were fast asleep (but woke up right away) when Georgina made an appearance. The apartment was immediately penetrated by the smell of perfume and cognac. Anna thought her aunt beautiful, mysterious, someone to look up to. But whenever her sister showed up, Maria lost no time in taking offence.

'She gives me this look that turns me into a maid.' Correct. Anna's father said nothing. 'And you won't say anything.' Correct. He was looking at his sister-in-law; it felt like they had left the window open, and a storm was forcing its way into the room – on a summer's night. Georgina was no more than twenty-five, but she looked thirty-five. She was heavily made up, her face slightly bloated, doughy, strange, strange,

strange. That's when he ran to the children's room, leaving the warring sisters behind, and buried his face in the blanket at Anna's feet, blubbering, as if he were innocent. Anna heard him in the dark and, repelled, pulled the pillow over her head, so she wouldn't have to be part of this shameful playacting. Why on earth would a grown-up cry? she thought, grown-ups should realize that there's nobody to comfort them. She was not afraid of her father, she detested him.

A few years previously, Georgina had been interned by mistake. It should have been the general next door, old Guido Beéry, whose apartment had a view from the hill on the Danube, while Georgina Béri lived in a room in the so-called superintendent's apartment, so it was quite unnecessary, really, to make her a subject of this historically so justified vigilance. But the early morning rains following St Medard's day in '51 had no consideration even for official documents. Besides, who could tell that Guido was not a woman's name? The mistake was quickly remedied, however, and they also took the general way.

Georgina had studied dance with great diligence; her soul and muscles were gifted enough, only her physique left something to be desired; it was of good proportions, but too short, too tight – this is where the diligence came in, to make up for something that could not be helped. She was taken to a village near Miskolc. In September, she stepped on a scythe. According to the family legend, the drunken guards held a sort of hunt, chasing after the 'whore from Pest', running from house to house; on that leaden afternoon she tried to hide and was hidden, but in the end there was nothing to do but run. A running girl with a panting horde at her heels. And then ... Thank God that these bigshots happened to be in the neighbourhood, she was taken by jeep to a hospital in Gyöngyös, the sharp steel cut through the sole of her foot right up to the ankle on one side, severed muscles, tendons, ligaments – a difficult but noble operation, said the doctor. This little episode hardly left a trace on the movements of former ballet student Georgina Béri.

'Is that really how it was?'

'Come, now, Anna, my pet. They wouldn't dare lay a finger on me. They just howled with desire from a distance, but they wouldn't dare lay a finger on me.' Georgina lied a lot. She started drinking after the operation. That was about thirty-five years ago.

'Why do you drink, Aunt Georgina?'

'I told you, my pet. Just call me Georgie. Don't be so formal, like that mother of yours. Who, as you know, couldn't stand the sight of me. But take my word for it, I never made a pass at your father. Though not because of your mother, either. And I don't just *drink*, I drink to excess . . . I've been drinking pitchers of beer for thirty-five years now, but not for the sake of drinking, no, I detest drunks, I drink because it helps me think, so I can get to the bottom of the text better, because I don't read for entertainment, merely to pass the time, or to help me fall asleep, I who live in a country where fifteen generation learned to read and write, I drink so that I should never again be able to fall asleep from reading, to make the act of reading send shivers up and down my spine, because I happen to share Hegel's view that a valuable person is rarely noble, and that a sinner is seldom a murderer. If only I could write, I would write a book about the great, great unhappiness of humankind, and it's great happiness . . .' ('Bohumil, now there's a gal for you! Beer and Hölderlin, they're your speciality.')

The second time Anna saw her father cry was in November 1956, when frightened but full of inane hope, he tried to draw encouragement from his daughter's eyes. The car was standing in front of the house, and the family all packed, her mother silent and glum in the kitchen, her father unable to come to a decision. He stayed behind out of cowardice, just as he would have gone out of cowardice – a Hungarian still-life, *anno domini* 1956, an icon: apartment after apartment, people waiting in the same way, with the same ashen complexions, the same suitcases, the same smell of gasoline coming from the waiting trucks, undecided fathers, silent, worried mothers, frightened children . . . (The Red Cross truck was standing in front of our house, too. Father sent the driver away without, perhaps, even looking up. It was only then that he said what I subsequently heard from him so often at soccer games, roared from inside, from the bleachers after a bad pass, What for? Where? Why? He said the same thing back then, too, on that bleak November morn, except more softly: What for. Where. Why.)

Anna did not know at the time – except for her father and Georgina, only the Good Lord knew – with whom his father had been on the phone that morning, and what he had said. Maria knew and did not know; what I mean is, she did not know, but it was just as if she did.

'That truly and unabashedly idiotic father of yours calls me that morning and says, let's go, just the two of us! Poor thing, through the years he took it into his head that he was in love with me. This was the only thing that was real in him, I might add, this imagined love for me. But don't you let on, dear. It's all the same now, anyway, there's nothing left. What a farce. The dead-serious imitation of the paraphase of self-parody: that's his life.'

'What? What was that?' the writer mumbled. 'What did you say?'

'Don't be so conceited. And don't think I was talking about you. Because I wasn't.'

'It never even entered my mind,' the writer said.

'Another exaggeration,' said Georgina, nodding into her beer. 'When the phone rang, I was hiding two people, a nineteen-year-old boy, a "revolutionary", but I don't want to talk about him now; the other was my girlfriend, who worked for the secret police . . . She was only a typist with the secret police. Still, far from immaculate. Her husband was a bona fide member of the corps. There's nothing I can do, there's nothing I can do, he kept saying to his wife, to my girlfriend, who also said the same thing to me, there's nothing I can do. She was retired at fifty with a nervous breakdown, back in '75. Been drinking quietly ever since.'

'With you?'

'No, Anna, my little flower, not with me. God's business is forgiveness. And man's business is remembering. Ethics is remembering . . . I mean . . . it's written that God made man in his own image . . . so man is not just an inconsequential *transition* . . . I forget, but I remember, too; I forgive, but I also take my revenge.'

The third time Anna heard and saw her father cry was eleven years after the second. Her father met, quite by chance, you might say, though it must be added that there are no chance happenings, or only rarely (*vide*: Christiann Huygens, who introduced the concept of *mathematical hope*; otherwise, though he lived only for science, he was not a recluse: he wrote poetry for the celebrated beauties of the time), he met a teacher from Sopron. Anna's brother found their letters two years before. 'Never in my life had I read such beautiful love letters, Bohumil. They were so virginal and dewy, and full of feelings that scared them, my father and that teacher, though they yearned so terribly . . . Just imagine . . . this . . . this elevated them to new heights, even grammatically. These letters are beautifully written. But my father backed down in face of the coming storm; our mother showed her muscle right away, used us as pawns, there we were, cowering in silence, two objects (points!) of reference, my brother scandalized, and me, crying, crying as I listened to my crying father, crying, because I never would have thought, and still do not, because I have forgotten what we saw then, that my father is a man of feeling, and – though he'd never showed the least sign of it – a real man.

'The next morning, our mother was sweet as honey. And more beautiful than ever. Who was she beautiful for? Not even for herself. After all, she did not even know that she was selfish. She never knew anything. Or is it just that I didn't know that she knew?

' "You take too many chances," she said when my husband and I were caught in the act.'

11

The Lord God, also known as the Good Lord, liked perlon stockings, he liked them individually, and he like them generally. For one thing, he considered them a refinement on the act of Creation, for another, he liked women's legs; nothing divine was alien to him, even though – and pardon my frivolity – he served part time as God of the Catholics, who have been known to denounce feminine charms. But the Lord God did not agree with this view, by which I do not in the least mean to imply that he identifies with me in every respect.

Not only was the quality of the Creation thus acknowledged retroactively – from the single-celled organism to the giraffe, from the two-stroke engine to the four-stroke engine – but in a way, eternity as well, and infinity: that's how long-wearing these stockings were, at least when compared to nylon products of recent times. Recent times: when (as God saw it) obsolescence and demise are designed into the making of objects (the example he liked to give was that a VW bug is still a VW bug after fifteen years, but what about a Golf after ten? Not to mention the Japanese products, or the rusting of a Fiat body) – these things he held against this emancipated end of the century, insisting, and I am all agreement here, that such matters were his business, his prerogative. He had half a mind to take this as an insult, but in the end settled for a minor earthquake at Skopje.

Only the infinite can be loved, they say. But the being who opines thus is finite. Can the infinite love the finite? Yes, indeed. The only proviso being that contemplation of our planet Earth at times visited a deadly, horrendous boredom upon the Lord. *Le silence éternel de l'espace infini m'effraie* (the eternal silence of infinite space fills me with dread) – Pascal, to be sure, was quoting the Lord. Most of all, it was the idyllic that bored him, bored him to tears, because that's when he was most on people's lips; but he especially resented all those references to his goodness. An idyll, according to the Greeks, is a small still-life, but an idyll is no small happiness. The Lord loved the small, as well as the happy; they are measured out in eternity, but the tight, the narrow-minded, the confined – these he could not abide.

'*O make me a mask,*' (Dylan Thomas) he sighed. Such were the games he played, a rainbow existence in an oil slick puddle. Behind the masks he remained the Merciful Lord, the most essential form of reality, which, however, it would be a mistake to take triumphantly, i.e., anthropomorphically, because, let's face it, he took his games *very* seriously. 'Gentlemen! He has different considerations!' a gigolo in

Hamburg was supposed to have said before sending a bullet into his brain. I read it somewhere, I swear.

He was also partial to the petty intrigues over perlon stockings that occurred in the sixth and seventh decades of the twentieth century, roughly, in the region of the Danube and the Ipoly. In addition to the perlon stockings, the other big hits were loosely knit mohair pullovers (or *sets*: pullover plus matching cardigan) and 'packamacs' or plastic raincoats – all of Central Europe (which back then was simply referred to as East Europe) rustled about in these. The Czech-Hungarian border crossings were full of life; on train after train human nature revealed itself in its myriad faces, tears and laughter, hatred and cunning, loyalty and treachery, yes, indeed! The gist of it was that in Chesko, it was cheaper. An old friend of mine told me the story – he had a grandpa who lost an arm to the threshing machine, the arm flew off, he found it, picked it up, wrapped it in newspaper, it must have been the *Free People*, I guess, then he slapped the package under the *other* arm, went to the hospital in Eger, and only then did he collapse – anyway, my friend says he stuffed some kind of folk embroideries all around his middle, he was going to trade them for perlon stockings, and he got busted, but one of the customs men happened to be a former student of his, he called his former teacher out of the compartment, and let him off with a sympathetic pat on the shoulder, sir, you shouldn't try this again, whereupon the teacher, sir!, started to swear so loud that the flowers wilted and the emergency brake went on. All this happened on the way there, and made him waste all the money his embroidered scarves brought on appeasing his blues over the humiliation and his all-too-hasty fright, so that he got terrifically plastered in the beautiful city of Prague – by recourse to one well-considered beer after another – so he never got to see the perlon stockings, nor the Hradcany

Palace, these illustrious vehicles of Czech culture. Beer is time, he realized, and said so. We ought to learn this much from the Czechs, he said.

We made mention of the epic nature of the Lord God, which in no way excluded a certain sensibility and a desire for dramatics on his part. Just think of the beautiful scenario, simple as pie (it would do credit to a competent French author of grade B music hall comedies), that, see, it is precisely the Chosen People who do not recognize the Saviour. A more demanding Author might possibly sneer at the notion, but he'd be way off the mark. The idea works. Every theatrical notion that works is a deeply human paradigm.

'Any creature can say *Ego*, but only God can say *sum* – I Am,' said the Lord, casting his moody eyes upon the writer from a great distance. He then began to whistle, together with Anna, Little Carlsson's 'Mini Pretty Teenie', a tune that, who knows why, never made it big; an equal mystery is why the same tune, in Jethro Tull's version of a different title, became an instant hit, although the band, with its customary jazz severity, made no concessions whatsoever.

12

Anna was just rolling the perlon stockings her father had (adventurously) acquired for her mother but which were unreasonably passed on to her, Anna, instead, up her muscular, youthful calves, when her mother's key jingled in the lock outside. Inside, it was Anna's key. And in her bed the writer, who at the time was not much of a writer; surely no more than a college boy.

Anna's parents did not like the boy. One look, and forthwith, they liked him not. It wasn't a *whole lot* that they did not like him, it was more like the shrug of the shoulders, really. 'He's not what you'd call prepossessing,' they told Anna when he was introduced, and this was more of a moral than an aesthetic condemnation. It was probably his otherness they could not deal with. When Anna went into detail about it, the writer was unaccountably seized by a wild fit of melancholy and was immediately deeply resentful besides – of Anna. He could not understand, he found it strange, he found it illogical – was in fact almost inclined to put it down to a streak of eccentricity in his in-laws that they appeared to be immune to snobbery, not to mention his growing reputation. Television, radio, neighbours, the butcher – nothing. Later, years later, his mother-in-law was relieved to see that her grandchildren were growing up all right – was bemused and surprised that her flighty daughter was still living with this flighty boy, ignoring all that might have disturbed her peace of mind.

As if they were living behind heavy sheet metal or lamination or a hard crust, that's how Anna regarded her parents' lives. There were no getting through to them. Then something her mother said on her deathbed opened her eyes; she realized (or came close to realizing) that she had never known the woman whom she deserted so easily for the sake of her mother-in-law, and who made this so easy for her.

'Your mother-in-law will tell you' – and in this there was no trace of bitterness. Everything was so transparent about her mother, her anger, her aches and pains, the sufferings that did not ring true, the tendentious hopes in a sea of indifference. Of that stunning and strong young girl on a 1938 family photo in a large-brimmed hat, wearing a gossamer flower-print dress of cotton billowing lightly in the summer breeze she did not think, she wiped it out of her memory, and it did not occur to her until the last moment by that bed.

Actually, the two youngsters in bed weren't even alarmed when they heard the puttering at the door. They giggled, two happy, scraggy adolescents. The girl was the sharper of the two.

'Quick! Get into your clothes!' Too late. The girl's mother stood in the door, at which, as if they had agreed beforehand, they shut their eyes. They shut them tight, like children, if I can't see you, you can't see me. Eventually they talked about this, and in fact, that's just what they were thinking. And seriously believing it, too, that it would help.

But it did not. And in an instant, everything just went from bad to worse.

'What do you think you're up to?'

The boy snuck under the douvet, from where he whispered, 'Should I tell her? Betcha she knows.'

The girl knew there was trouble, she knew her mother's face, this greying of the surface, the cruel set of the lips, the cutting edge of her pulpy voice.

'I think I feel sick,' the boy added in a whiny voice, so inane it surprised even him. The bed, the associative basis, that's what did it! The mother tore her daughter from the bed, she pulled the douvet with her, at which the boy, plucked naked, wrapped himself in the sheet, no easy feat when you happen to be lying on top, a classical situation. As he got dressed, he could hear the fight flare up outside. Anna's voice calmed him. When he appeared through the door, the woman's anger soared to new heights. She started drubbing the boy with both fists. And he miscalculated again, thinking they were over the rough spots (that the thing has losts its edge, because when we're standing on the edge of a thing, the thing loses its edge), and grabbing the diminutive woman's wrists, arresting her blows in mid-air, as it were, kissing 'mother's' hands, and grinning, repeating over and over again, 'Stop it will ya? Stop it already.'

He was barred from the house for many years. 'You precious Czech man, of a surety you must have suffered a sea of sadness and torment, for you were made to suffer them; around these parts a good man and true might as well think of adversity and vilification as part of his birthright. Golden Prague, silken Budapest, honeyed Belgrade, iron Bucharest, chiming Vienna, life pulled to shreds, then stuck together again. I know. All the same, I bet you've never had your virginity *looked* into. Worse than the regime. Poor dad dragged me to the Health Service doc, why he bothered I'll never know. I could've told them right then and there that I'd given my virginity to this college boy three days before, and I'm glad I didn't get cold feet, even though I was so scared, I trembled before, and I trembled after. Before we left he had a thorough out-and-out with mother in the kitchen, behind closed doors, I could clearly make out the word whore, and it felt good, not knowing if the reference was to me or my mother. But waiting my turn on the white bench was the pits, dad sitting by my side, lips buttoned up, and too late to make amends. He went in ahead of me to speak to the doc whom he knew, and who, when we were alone, stroked my head, it's all right, child, it's all right. This got me crying, I put my arms around this stranger, and bawled and bawled. He never examined me.'

'You can go now,' he said glancing at his watch. 'And take care of yourselves.' He sighed. 'Today was the last time I called you child.'

When the girl stepped out of the doctor's office, a heavenly voice spoke up.

'All hell to pay, Cho-Cho, old boy?'

The doctor removed his spectacles, and like all who wear glasses, massaged the bridge of his nose.

'All's well, Big Boss. Just the usual stuff. Dignity and stupidity, weakness and idiocy, like always. It's smoothed over, though, the wounded are being seen to.'

'I'm not good at anything except love,' Anna said defiantly to her mother when she got home. The statement was modest only superficially, for it squared with Plato's own, who, as the always reliable Tura was kind enough to point out for us, conceived of love as the sole aim of the universe, the primal striving for unity.

'You take too many chances,' her mother said in a tone of reconciliation.

At the time she just shrugged, but later, by the side of the bed which you could not know would be a deathbed, she had to think of something else besides; that a lack of daring is not necessarily cowardice, and that by itself, daring is not always of value. Could she have been looking at her mother from far too great a distance? She, Anna, wanted to take nothing for granted, nothing that her circumstances forced on her, circumstances, habits, conventions, developments, the country, Eastern Europe. Possibly, her mother is an East-European, a poor European, bear your burden, resign yourself, salvage what you can, comply and submit, a woman who knows where she is living, look, little one, don't be a fool, have you any idea where you are living? listen to no one, listen to your mother, lie low, stoop, drag your burden along, do what you can, do what they'll let you, if they ask a lot of questions don't say anything, if they cross-question you confess, confess everything, except don't tell on anyone living, don't tell on your enemy, but do confess that you spied for de Gaulle in favour of King Charles, then with an about-face against him, and former Prime Minister Károlyi is your

contact in the upper echelons, that while in kindergarten you
cleverly recruited an army, the reason is obvious enough,
confess that hidden inside some chocolate you passed secret,
forged documents to the Comintern, confess that you are
Rosa Luxemburg, that Rajk held no fascination for you as a
man, confess that you wrote 'The End of September' because
you are the poet Petőfi's Russian wife, you think it's all
nonsense by now, don't you, a good joke, you'll never know
when they're joking, never, their minds are not like ours, so
you'd better not go around this country just like that, don't
think you own it, you can see who owns it, be the first to say
hello, my precious, to each one you say hello first, it's not you
you'll be demeaning, as for the country, it'll be overgrown
with grass, don't feel bad about it, it was always like this, it is
like this now, and so it shall remain, lie low, don't say what
you're thinking, and don't even think what you won't say,
what's the use, don't let them confuse you, you don't know
yet what they're like, but I do, and if a kind-hearted young
soldier suggests you cry because that'll save your life, never
mind what kind of life, it's life! then cry, sob, pinch yourself
till you bleed, rub your eyes, scrub them till the tears come, if
they won't let you wash, rip a swatch out of your skirt, don't
spare it, don't spare any of your skirts, to survive, to outlive
them, no matter how, that's all that matters, they took
twenty-eight men from the street and not one came back, I
may be just a silly old woman, little one, but believe me, I
know what I'm talking about, can't you see, the mere fact that
we are alive is a divine miracle, during the past fifty years
anyone here had a good chance of dying, here there is no
shelter, nothing to fall back on, nothing to defend yourself
with, you can't outwit them, you've got to keep your eyes
open though and have your wits about you, so when it's time
to turn in the requisitioned lard you take them lard from

the innards, which stinks to high heaven, so you've got to cover it with paper-thin strips of real lard, it's not easy but you'll learn, darling, you must learn to cope, like the beasts of the wild learn the hidden paths, the traps, which way the wind blows, and learn about the hunter, too, you can't get around it, we're *past* that, fear for your life and hide and keep quiet until they grow extinct to the last man, ravenous dogs, that's what they're like, so throw them a bone, your silence, your acquiescence, let them gulp it down, gorging themselves on our tears and our silence, devouring it with both cheeks so they won't have time to think, let them lie out in the sun with bulging stomachs, there'll be peace at least while they're at it, hold your tongue, you'll have children some day, and what'll become of them, and my darling, don't believe what this boy tells you either, don't listen to him, listen to your mother! who is he anyhow? a haughty fool, freedom? what the hell is he talking about? what freedom? *the two weeks plus the extras?* the extra days, that's freedom, they're taping everything he says and playing it back, sometimes fast forward, sometimes slowed down, and they howl with laughter over it in there, that's what you should be thinking about, the tapes as they're howling over them, don't trust him, he's nothing but pleasant words now, promising you the moon, talking big, showing off, but they're different, different from us, little one, they're privileged, rich, even if they happen to be out of money, even if they get kicked around, like us, you should be afraid of him, too, they're big shots, thinking they can rule the world, thinking it's all there for the asking, thinking they can use the world, refusing to announce anything, they're spoiled adolescents, inquisitive, shameless, afraid of no one, they're rich, no, no, and he can't protect you, shooting his mouth off won't do it, protecting you is one thing he can't do, because there is no protection to be had, and this boy does not know and never will, he doesn't even *want* to know, and maybe there is no reason why he should know how to bear his share of the burden, to resign himself, to salvage what he can, to comply and submit, don't believe him, don't believe him.

Anna did not believe her mother but did believe this boy (at times, in fact, it was she the boy believed). But possibly her mother knew what was going on? What her choices were? Possibly she accepted something as her own, possibly her story is not of muteness but of silence? History that has gone unwritten, speech without words, beauty beyond the bounds of art, truth beyond man . . .

The dying woman spoke thus:

'When you buy fur, little Anna, have a razor blade with you, and when the salesman is not looking, split it open on the side. If it's blue it's OK, because of the indigo, but if it's grey, you mustn't buy it, even if it suits you, because it will shed its fur. That's what happened to the gynaecologist in Szolnok, the one I was in love with. *All* of Szolnok, I might add, was in love with him.'

And she also said: 'How many things we write off to love . . . how much destruction . . . with the best of intentions . . . Something hasn't been thought through here, something hasn't been thought through in us, the Good Lord did not think it through . . . For all I know, the Good Lord may not have been thought through properly either . . . Yes, I think I made the right choice, little one.'

13

Our stories are bound together by fear and patriotism. Correction. Our stories are bound together by fear rather than patriotism. Correction. What we call patriotism is really our fear. This constitutes our story. The writer stretched, just like a well-fed child. Cho-Cho was not too crazy about him, having known him for quite a while. (Before Cho-Cho, an angel named Martin Susan Kovács had the assignment, but was busted after being caught, together with his partner, taking high school girls for joyrides while on duty.) Not that Cho-Cho had any problems with the writer; the only thing he didn't like about him was the fact that he wrote – the flood of words, the ink drying on the page, that sort of thing. And he knew why. Because all of this bore an uncanny resemblance to his own life. Angels have no life of their own. And the writer wasn't even an angel.

I got a hold of Don Aldbarth Elmewitsch's text on angels. It was sent to me by the translator, Franciska Frisova, herself – no, not an angel! more like a Central European picture book, or, to use an old social phrase, *K. und K. mischung*: Croatian (Bulgarian?) grandparents, mother from Prague, who-knows-what-part Jewish father from Austria (and what does it mean, to be 'Austrian'?); for a while she was married to my younger brother, who claims he fell in love with Frisova because she'd *always* know of a good second-hand shop in the neighbourhood where fantastic blouses(!) could be had, which made my brother conclude that this held the promise of a fine and colourful life together. Needless to say, this *idée fixe* of my brother's toward Frisova soon showed its *true* colours.

This Novi Sad scholar, repatriated from Kiev, well deserved the monicker Doctor Angelicus, or Doctor Angel-orum, thereby emphasizing the uncircumventability of St Thomas Aquinas. (I received news of his death the other day. God be with you, Don . . .) Don – because that's how he is referred to in the profession, as well as 'the Old Man' – had started out from the commonly held view that God is dead, a fertile notion, though far from the truth. As evidence to the contrary, consider, if nothing else, the frequent flashes of the Lada's gear-shift stick, and the non-stop ukases it emanates. Ever since the invention of the walkie-talkie, there is no keeping the Lord down; *someone* (to put it jocosely) is always on the line. It was with a sense of superiority that Cho-Cho thought of the deists. They surely bungled this one (not that he relished the constant vexation), but what's an angel to do? (Toward atheists, on the other hand, he felt distinctly sympathetic, and a *tenderness* for the godless; on the other hand, he could not understand those who denied God: if he does not exist, what's the use of denying him, and if he does, how can he be denied? By the way, I feel the same thing about this – and oh, yes, about women's lib.)

So: the death of God left the angels in a particular (or peculiar; the synonyms are Frisova's interjection, reflecting her – and to some extent the text's – uncertainties) situation. Just picture it – what they must have *looked* like (what a fine figure they must have cut) at the moment when that basic question surprised them (bowled them over); you could have knocked them down with a feather as their angelic consciousness was filled, and themselves subdued with frightening impact. And the question, for there is no getting around it, was this: What are angels?

The question of what angels 'are' (the quiddity of angels) has a considerable history (literature). Swedenborg, for one, conversed with a whole lot (a whole *bunch*) of angels, and took accurate notes on what they told him. And he saw, time and time again, that angels are like people – saw (needless to say), not with his physical, but with his spiritual eyes.

Swedenborg has a great deal to say, of the highest interest: that no angel is permitted to stand behind another and look at the back of his head, for this would disturb (interfere with) the influx (flood) of goodness and truth from the Lord; that

73

angels have their eyes perpetually trained to the east because that is where the Sun is; and that they are clothed (robed) according to their intelligence, the most intelligent among them bedecked (as it were) in blazing tongues of flame, others in glimmering light, and less intelligent ones in garments of various colours (resplendent with a multitude of colours). But the angels of innermost heaven are unclothed (naked)!

All of this, presumably, no longer obtains.

Gustav Davidson, in his useful (invaluable) monograph, has brought (heaped) together much of what is known about angels. (Davidson: *A Dictionary of Angels*, New York and London, 1967). Their names are as follows: the angel Alubatel (or Elutabel), the angel Friagne, the angel Gaap, the angel Hatiphas (genius of finery), the angel Murmur (a fallen angel), the angel Mqttro, the angel Or, the angel Rash, the angel Sandalphon (longer than a walking tour of five hundred years, though here something may have been lost in the translation), and the angel Smat. Davidson distinguishes (establishes) categories: Angels of Quaking (Tremor), who surround the heavenly throne; Masters of Howling and Lords of Shouting, whose task is praise; messengers, mediators, watchers, warners (encouragers, intercessors, monitors and admonitors). To which I wish to add the names of the following angels: Bruno Ganz and Otto Sander of Berlin, and Blaise, and Cho-Cho.

In his 1957 study entitled 'The Psychology of Angels', Joseph Lyons provides the most exquisitive account of the angel lore of former times. Lyons is convinced (he avers) that every angel knows everything that can conceivably be known about himself or another angel. Angelic existence is a compact, self-contained system and no angel can be more or less than another angel. Joy and horror in one and the same pair of eyes: this is the angel. To be caught in the middle: this accounts for the hysterical nature of temptation. Angels do not ask questions, because questions arise from not-knowing (acknowledged not-knowing). Angels are not curious, either; they have nothing to be curious about. In this respect, they differ from the Lord, and from humans, too. Nor are they amazed at anything. Knowing everything there is to know, the world of all possible knowledge, to an angel, must appear as an ordered set of facts (structures) which, so to speak, said angel has perfectly surpassed and left behind, and which he holds securely in the grasp of his hand . . . HUMAN UNCERTAINTY IS ABOUT THE WORLD HELD IN THIS HAND; GOD'S UNCERTAINTY IS ABOUT THE HAND ITSELF.

But this, too, no longer obtains.

It is a curiosity of writing about angels that very often one turns out to be writing about men (humans). The themes (topics) are twinned. (The subjects overlap.) Thus, one finally learns (it becomes obvious, at long last) that Lyons, for instance, is really writing about schizophrenics. He is thinking about men when he mentions angels – not an infrequent occurrence in the literature on the subject; a point, so our Don, that was not lost on the angels (having animated them) when they began considering their new relationship to the cosmos, when the analogues (is an angel more like a quetzal, or more like a man? or more like music?) were handed our (bandied about).

Elmewitsch goes on to hypothesize with considerable *élan* (oomph) that the basis for self-determination was provided (established) by the work at hand. An angel is what he (it) does. Thus arose the need to investigate (look for) new roles. (You are reminded that what follows is impure speculation.) After the lamentation had gone on for hundreds and hundreds of whatever the angels use for time, an angel proposed that lamentation be the function of angels eternally, as adoration had been formerly. Furthermore, the mode of lamentation would be silence – this in contract to the ceaseless (endless) singing (chanting) of Glory; on the other hand (of course), silence is contrary to the basic nature of angels.

A counter-proposal was that angels affirm (justify?) chaos. There were to be five great (terrific, whopping) proofs of the existence of chaos, of which the first was the absence (withdrawal) of God. The other four were not in evidence, but surely, they too could be located somewhere or other. On the other hand (of course), there is not much enthusiasm for chaos among angels (angels evince only a moderate enthusiasm for chaos).

The most serious, because more radical, proposal entertained by the angels was the refusal (full denial) – that they would remove themselves from being (withhold themselves from existence). Not be. The tremendous (horrendous) dignity (exaltedness) that would accrue to the angels by this act was felt (held) to be a manifestation (evidence) of spiritual pride: the negation of negation.

There were other suggestions as well, more subtle and complex (or less so), but none overwhelmingly attractive (irresistably tantalizing).

I saw a famous angel on television; the light veritably dripped from his robes. The situation of angels today was his topic. Angels, he was saying, are, in a certain manner of speaking, just like men (humans), and the problematics of adoration are decisive (central). He related how angels have tried out adoring (worshipping) each other, just as we are doing ourselves, but in the long run, this proved (was concluded to be) 'not enough' ('inadequate'). So they are going to continue the search for a new principle (idea), he said.

And with that, let us take our leave of the great Don. By the way, according to my brother (but he was drunk when he said this) Frisova ruined his life. On the one hand, he's hated her ever since, with an unabating fervour, and on the other, he cannot forget her, she just won't go out of his mind. When he sees her, every two or three years, on the street in Prague, Vienna, or Budapest (and once in Sibiu, Romania), he becomes sick, his stomach heaves, and regardless of what he has had to eat, he's got to throw up. Poor thing. And he's married again, has two small children, as far as I can see he loves his work, there he is appreciated.

Cho-Cho was listening to a saxophone quartet on a casette a certain Colonel Sándor gave him. Thomas Waczy, father of the Czech saxophone (and mother of the Slovak clarinet), writes somewhere: 'What we cannot express in music, we must make into "non-music", for there has to be *some* music . . .'

He was dead tired. The people in the neighbourhood now refused to greet him out of familiarity. All the angel wanted to do was to complete his task. He was what he did. The Lord is all, man is a grain of sand – at the moment, both of these seemed attractive possibilities. He was no longer pulling for Anna, he no longer desired that they should not fall into sin, nor did he wish for the opposite, neither good nor bad, nor any surprises, either, though that was a good sign. But he did not want any good signs either. He did not like to stay on earth for very long. He was trying to formulate his report. Lord, it is time. Your summer has dragged on long enough. Or: Enough, Lord. Your summer, it hath been a drag. Or: Get on the ball, Lord. And kiss your summer good-bye. You mean *summertime*, Cho-Cho, old pal, *summertime*, the Big Boss will probably say.

Anna swept down the length of the street like a typhoon. If all goes well, if . . ., then all you have to do is wait until evening and it'll be over . . . But where is Blaise? He always missed little Blaise, even when the latter was right by his side. Cho-Cho was over thirty and he was becoming more and more shameless, no matter how he fought against it. Angels come and angels go. He had to laugh when he recalled that Anna had come pretty close to becoming an 'angel-maker', an abortionist, herself. (Where is your innocence? I am not saying that it is lost, but I ask you: where is it? a friend of his had once asked.)

Blaise appeared in the greyish-blue twilight. As you know, angels are large and white. But at this moment, Blaise seemed to be brownish, and surely no taller than six feet. He did not get into the car but only sat down sideways, like girls in Rome on their mopeds, his back to his friend. There was a long silence, even by angelic standards of time. Cho-Cho could not take his eyes off the back of the younger angel's neck, but let's not go into that. Did he take care of the obstetrician? Were there any complications? Well, then, they might as well get going, having accomplished their task for the greater glory of God. Blaise started to squawk and scream like an old crone, a veritable hag. 'I am the slave of light! The salesman of enlightenment! The henchman of illusion.' He was panting. 'The coolie of radiance.'

'You've been drinking,' said Cho-Cho with a sigh, but Blaise did not hear this, he was an angel no more. Anna was all he could think of, her shapely legs, the arch of her back, and he even imagined a silky little pantie, and focused on that. I miss you, I miss you! Blaise found he was missing something; he was inadequate unto himself, this is why he missed Anna so; he could find embodiment in himself, but not Anna in him. Or something like that. These last few days he made use of every cheap theatrical trick, from becoming invisible to appearing in the guise of Alain Delon, just so Anna would notice him. Even his heart beat faster. He imagined, romantically and incorrectly, that the humming inside his bowels was the song of the seraphim. Not entirely disinterested, Cho-Cho lent him a shoulder to cry on.

Oh that woman, that Anna, she's an angel. Or at the very least, descended from angels. Her freckles prove it, they're the imprint of the sun. Freckled people were creatures of light. He imagined her in a ball gown, their faces a playground of heartfelt emotion as they move to soft music . . . Against your will, against your will, I, he whispers into her ear, and she laughingly nods assent, yes, yes, that's how it will be, against my will, and she caresses the boy's face, and he hers, her nose, her lips, all those golden freckles. Suddenly he nestles his face in between her breasts. Blaise did his best to think like a man. He even made the appropriate faces.

There came a light drizzle in the dark. Man and wife were in bed, the issue of the unborn child smoothed over in a Christian spirit, and as for the neighbourhood, it would sigh in relief once 'that secret police car' had left. Cho-Cho, who could not decide whether to disparage or praise Blaise's determination, bestowed a feathery kiss on the back of his head. They would not look each other in the eye. Blaise slammed the car door shut, the Lada leaped into the air, and disappeared among the clouds. Old man Kondász put down his pint of beer. A police car in the air? He waved it off; nothing surprised him any longer. Obviously, they must have come up with yet another gimmick . . .

Little Blaise, the apprentice from next door, strolled out to the street corner, and leaning against the pole black with grime, took great sighing drags on his cigarette. When he flicked it away, the red glow of the butt on the wet road went out with a hiss, and died, and yet . . . and yet, that cigarette butt was the centre of the world (and still is).

The Chapter of Infidelity

'I have never seen a woman quite so naked before'
from a Moravian prayer in
Less Would Have Been More, Prague, 1958

Dear Bohumil,

ya kvahm piishu chevo zhe bolyeh
shtoh ya mahgu yischo skazhaty . . .

Do forgive me for vexing you.
I (we?) have been too lax with respect to time.

I would love to have an exchange of letters with you. I
imagine the way our letters would *cross* each other. – Dear
Bohumil, I am not talking about you; the best thing you can do
is have a good laugh at my expense. One part of me trusts men
like that (such *laughing* men), another part of me is offended.

Would you like me to blackmail you? 'A letter is such a
terrible nothing, and it can say such an awful lot,' Attila József
wrote this a few weeks before his suicide. I am going to stick
you inside an envelope.

It is night, a complicated time of day.
Things might go smoother.

I did some feeding. Two of my husband's friends came over. (Those precious dears.) That makes three handsome men. And each so different. I love them, the way they differ like this. Especially these two. I like to hug them, too. (One's got a beard that smells of the earth. A grass roots *Magyar*, no doubt.) And it's not just the good smell either; they're worth cooking for.

My mother-in-law had a deep-seated contempt of recipes, and taking my cue from her, so do I. Though she had her reliable staples, the legendary *cutlet with sardella paste* or the *sauce picante* she served with meat (a simple mixture of jam and mustard), and I also like to play it safe now and then, and bake a well-seasoned pork chop; still, even though I have favourites, they never turn out the same way twice. I am so capricious only because I don't *know* how to be the same; my many-sidedness is my limitation. Whether something turns out a lemon cake or a *bouillabaisse*, well, that is decided strictly *en route*.

Actually, we're lucky with this 'I cook like her and I don't'; this way, I am his mother-instead-of-his-mother, and I am not. – Basically, only the goulash is a source of conflict. His mother, she made it differently. How differently? Well, she did this and she did that, sliced the potatoes *lengthwise*, for one thing. Fine. All right. But still, it's not the same. Want me to throw it in the fire? Don't be silly. Do you like it? Oh yea, a lot. In which case, I have a suggestion: let's not call it goulash. But it is goulash, he says, all wide-eyed innocence. No, it is not; it is a triangle, or an apple tart. He glares at me. Fine. He nods solemnly. (No wonder if people are a *bit* taken

81

aback on hearing, 'did you put enough hot peppers in the apple tart?' . . .)

A long time ago (ten years, to be exact), I would have liked to give *soirées*, keep an open house, have Chinese lanterns in the garden, and all the neighbours free to come and go, drop in, even the ones I can't abide (either because they're two-faced or because I am unfair with respect to them). We'd have old-fashioned bakes, not those barbecue parties; I'd show off my prowess instead with a traditional bacon roast; suddenly, the whole block would discover 'the richness of simple things': the defrocked priest with the exemplary family life, the old maid, the widower with five children, the former council president, whom the rebels in '56 forced up to the roof of the city council building, even though he was the same old man back then, weighing two-hundred pounds, would he kindly bring down that reddish star with his two bare hands, and he scampered up and brought it down, and his hair went white when he handed it over, it went white on the spot. He's been sitting in his room ever since, he never shows, doesn't even get up, not even for a glass of water, even that his grandson has to take him. I can never get up the nerve to ask his daughter after him. According to the Báránys, he's long since dead. Before the war Laci Bárány's father owned a restaurant by the Danube, his father would stand out garden on the landing stage, waiting for the fishermen with their fresh catch, and he would point at the fish by name, I'll have Frankie-boy there, and this little Mary here. He was on such good terms with the fish.

When we first moved here, they accepted us as adults only reluctantly, little by little, gradually, they were so used to seeing my husband as a boy; my father-in-law remained our neighbour who, on the rare occasions that he came over, thoughtlessly wolfed down my cooking, and with cool amicability initiated his son and grandson into the mysteries of *der-die-das*, and stopped for a chat with the neighbours at the garden gate. Mighty neighourly of him. – It was the lamp-light that did it. Because whenever people came home on our street, at eight in the evening or one at night, on foot, half drunk or sober, by taxi, the lamp was burning in my darling's room. Did they forget to turn it off? By autumn, when the garden hedge had lost its leaves, the mystery was solved: they saw the son of the gentleman next door, there he was, hunched over his desk. What's he up to? (Biting his pen, that's what.) A tough one to answer. At this point it was the children that shed light on the matter. I was OK, they saw me sweating, panting, tottering under the weight of my shopping bags, this they understood. The son of the gentleman next door is the husband. So he must be their provider. Makes money for them, for the wife and kids. In which case, there by the lamp, at night, that must be some sort of work or something, after all. Which makes them hard-working people. Eccentric, hard-working people.

Our neighbours seldom visit us (thank the Lord), and one's friends are also thinning out, especially the would-be-friends, the half-friends, of whom we have so many in our younger days, and all so *promising*. But now one hand will suffice should I want to count them.

You know Bozhek what it's like living in this regime for forty years. Well . . . how shall I put it, it's no good. The heroes, of course, have grown fat everywhere during these forty years. I happened to hear them from the kitchen. If the European tradition, whose custodians are the men, is in trouble, and even before the dessert comes they conclude that value is something that has to be *created*, something new, then the situation of a kitchen-sink angel like myself is congenial, after all. I hum a song and think of God, about how things are. About the way time had slowed down, no longer sweeping me along, in the morning you must know what's to be done and why, day by day you must learn to face your demon, because you look into the mirror, and you ask, why? and you are greeted by silence. When I lean my head to the side, I see the flesh shifting one way, then the other and back again, like people in a boat panic-stricken lest they sink too fast. That this regime makes people feel even more isolated. That against its destructive forces you have only yourself to pit, we have no traditions to justify our reflexes, we have no *partners* because of this. That Fontane, now, he had it easy, he belonged, he had *grounds* for being at peace.

They also had a drink or two. Intimidated by the two serious men, my joy in life blinked nervously. Worse, he blinked logically. I could see him sliding lower and lower in the armchair (I had found it discarded! Bohumil! If ever you need a woman for clearing away junk, I'm the one!), I could see that he had no *ready* opinion again, how awfully hard he was listening, hoping to pick his friends' brains. He said something that made his friend laugh, the one I love now more than anything, and said, 'It's your way of getting off scot-free. And it's valid. You're forgetting one thing, though. That *everybody*, everybody can't get off scot-free.' – And he was still laughing, not a forced but a bitter laugh, as almost always. At times I can see how lonely he is, and it can't be helped. There is nothing to be done.

Sometimes when I get up, when I begin to surface from my sleepy torpor, the whole place hurts, my entire room, the view from the window hurts, the children going to school, people going off to buy their groceries, they all have some place to go except for me, I have no place to go, I get dressed in a daze, reeling, skipping on one foot, stepping on my pants as I pull them on – this is what you write, Bohumil, and that you don't like looking at yourself in the eye any more, that by now even the sight of your own self hurts, and you are horrified by what you see in the bathroom.

So be it. Be horrified. Why look in the mirror? Let me do the looking for you. On a day like this I'd show up at your place in Prague (while – oh, banal and clumsy fate – my husband would be writing about you and Prague back home). I've cleaned up, you'd say by way of greeting. I'd conduct a lightning-quick survey, and what have we here, find a half-slip dangling in the bathroom window, like a woman's body, part of a body, a fragment from the crotch to the breasts, as if you had no need of anything else; with a frown you'd take the petticoat and, without so much as a sideways glance, fling it out the window. Murderer, I'd smile flirtatiously, offering myself without much compassion for members of my sex.

Or possibly, I wouldn't find you at home. You'd be out on the town. I wouldn't give a damn about Prague, 'the golden Prague of enchantment, the Queen of Cities, the quaint quarters, the narrow streets leading into the past'; I would only care about you. I'd go bonkers over you, Hrabachek. I'd scour every tavern in pursuit; you wouldn't be at the Otta, and you wouldn't be at the Poison Green either, nor at the Golden Tiger. Should I go look for you in Fish Street, at the Hotel Central? Or at the Hajenka Restaurant, in the forest of Kersko? But that might be a bit over the top, perhaps. I'd be the only woman at the U Pinkasŭ, where they'd eye me plenty, but you wouldn't be there either. As the old Slovak saying goes, warm beer won't fatten you.

Lost: one male golden retriever, he is old and he limps and he has a nasty temper.
Computer network programmed removal of débris in dumpsters.

Call us with confidence! Rock-climbing work-group (private enterprise) will remove political emblems that have outlived their usefulness. Full discretion, no charge. Replies to 'Silly Billy'.

Mixed bag of bio-worms for sale, just 18–20 *fillérs*.

(This I have read especially for you.)

I had a dream about you.

But no more about my dreams, why vex him, when he should be doing the dreaming about you. As for you, instead of organizing colourful and erotic dreams, you are delivering *important* speeches.

About how if it has been raining in a country for decades or longer, pouring, coming down in torrents, drizzling, misting in fine droplets, and everything we have is already soaked through, our clothes, our shirts, our shoes, our eyes, our brains, our bones, our *pomp and glory*, our *mythologies*, and the panties of the women are mouldy with the damp and their bras musty, then this rain is *there* – it cannot not be there – it is everywhere, in the music, the paintings, the novels, it is *on the scene*, everywhere; not that it necessarily has to be raining in the novels, there the sun can shine to its heart's content, but that is a different sunshine, a rainy sunshine. We write one way in the rain, and another way when the sun shines. In the rain, the protagonists die faster.

Another time it's the blankets. How *those*, and it is clear who you mean, that those up in Prague take our blankets away and give us back shorter ones in return, so that our arms and legs, shaking and shivering, stick out. Still, it's better than nothing. And before we know it, our children grow up with the idea that this left-over, this hand-out – that this is what is called a blanket, that this is indeed a blanket, these scraps.

That a blanket has always been like this, made so our feet should stick out. Then next they take the remnant they call a blanket away from our kids, so that later still we should call the remnant of the remnant a blanket. And we know from Zeno's paradox that there will always be some blanket left. That is the essence of socialism.

In the morning it occurred to me that I had heard all this from my father-in-law once. I'm getting you ageing, fantastic men mixed up.

I also had a dream about you in which you disappeared without a trace. By the morning, nothing but one sentence remained. The world is not getting worse, only less innocent. A good sentence.

No use. No use playing for time, hiding it, hiding myself, staying out of sight, chattering and blubbering, something's gone wrong, Bohumil. And that something is that I didn't get my period. But don't worry. Not that you're the worrying type. How would a lady put it? A real, bona fide lady from Prague? *Eine Dame aus Prag*? One that's seen Kafka. My lunar clock is off? Fine. Bohumil, my pet, there appears to be a problem athreatening my person, my lunar clock is off.

What kind of an old gal will I make, I wonder? As a woman I pass, but I will make a rotten old bitch, way, way below par. My mother-in-law and her bunch were the last of the old guard who even past seventy were scrupulously attentive to the coordination of watch-band and scarf, shoe and handbag, weather and lipstick, mood and skirt length, make-up and foreign policy, and if everything was not – because it could not be – in order, they were *painfully* aware of it. The very idea of imitation leather made them faint and run a fever, and they never said 'samwich' and 'see-ya-round'. They had the pride of the captain of an ocean liner: This is my ship, this is my realm, I am in charge here, I can avert evil and promote the good. I do not for a moment believe that only my mother-in-law and her beautiful creole-skinned sister, those two grand ladies, were like that, I see such 'mercilessly pulled together' old people tip-toeing around town, 'pulled together' to just this side of the ridiculous.

They will die out. Finding fish every Friday, now that is something to lean on. I don't know what I am going to lean on. These hats and shawls, these modes of greeting, these *vacuous* forms, I'm not saying that they tell us anything about fate, Bohumil, but about a kind of life in which there was order. Probably not God's order any more, but a world in which everything had its appointed place, it may not have been just, and free only within limits, but you could get your bearings. That is over now.

I've done a lot of thinking about your mother. And now I even saw a picture of her. Everything you wrote is true, I see. It would have been nice asking her about things, things, too, that you, my dear, neglected to ask, if you don't mind me saying . . .

I don't *watch* anything I do, I just sort of do it. There is some good in this, I know, but what happens, what will happen, should both the watching and the doing stop? . . .

My mother-in-law's sister: 'So then, my child, in marched those nice Russians, right? I refused to get trapped in that *cul-de-sac* of whether they raped your husband's aunt, what I mean is, she's no relative but your husband's uncle's wife, I mean ex-wife, so then, whether she was raped or was just asking for it, in any case, at the time a certain unbiased expectation was not only understandable and justified, but compulsory as well. Yes. If only I had had a red handkerchief when the first Ivans appeared on our street. Or nail polish. But nothing. Nothing red. What a breach of etiquette. Just the blood flowing from my nose, soon after . . .'

Kittens in the forest of Kersko. And you, feeding them. It's nice, thinking about it. There are days, Bozho, sort of nothing days, I go get all dolled up as if I were going to a dance. But I only go out to the kitchen and do the dishes. When my husband comes in he looks on for a while in silence. Tell me, do I remind you of the rabbi's daughter from Bratislava, the one you loved and who loved you, that Perla? Come tomorrow, and I'm having this baby scraped out of me.

The last time I was pregnant was when we moved into this house; we had to sell the smaller one first, there was a couple, the prospective buyers, there was no doubt about the seriousness of their intentions, everything was set, we had even agreed on the price, they didn't give us a down payment, and we didn't ask for one, I was already negotiating with the wife over the details, the curtains yes, the benches no, and what are the neighbours like; the wife was a judge, my husband asked her once, he asked every woman judge he met, how many today? how many did she have shot that day? and he grinned, thinking he was being clever, but a deep silence followed, the next day the wife showed up to take some measurements for the combination wardrobe, she was slightly tipsy, I guessed cognac, and so I brought her cognac right away, even though I much prefer plum brandy, I always know of a couple of 'sources' where I can get lovely, clear, powerful brandy; the minute she saw we were alone the words came pouring out, later my husband heard the whole thing from me again, aghast, how something *always comes to light* here, what he means is, not something, but always the same thing, though the whole country is swathed in silence, the dead men's feet still sticking out of the ground, how for decades they had executed nearly a hundred men every hour, one or two per minute on the average, so that if the Central Headsman grew slack now and again, because he was watching TV or talking to his mother, death had to swing his scythe overtime not to fall behind schedule, how these stories come *slithering* out, like earthworms, like spotted hyenas, how it's slowly getting to him, said my precious, fear is all he's got left, really, no time left to be attentive, compassionate, or outraged, and my husband was right to feel this way, it's what the judge was saying herself, let's have a little cognac, for the judge's brother was still in high school when the ÁVÓ took him away, they nailed his balls, excuse me, dear, to the desk – motifs for a folk tale, Bohush, love, for these men pissing in the mouth, nailing to desks, tearing out fingernails, that's what's become of the seven-headed dragon and the king's youngest son – as if they were his own, that's how her brother loves her children, but that's not the point, but who do you think led the interrogation? none other than the brother's best friend from school who a while back, from conviction, because he wanted to serve his people, because his family was very poor before the war and his father died of tuberculosis in '42, because there was no money for a good doctor, he joined the secret police, and now they were trying him out to see if he'd be suitable for more important assignments, so there they stood face to face – 'maths test tomorrow!' – the schoolmate trembling, her brother trembling, too, from fear, one the torturer, the other the tortured, and that this schoolmate, where's that cognac? her brother's multilator, is her husband! – Why are you telling me this? Don't be so formal with me. Please. You can trust me! Let's have another cognac. My husband was retired early. We had you checked out. You have nothing to worry about. What're you talking about? Oh, nothing, I assure you, nothing, and then she started crying, sobbing without tears, drooling, shaking hysterically, she put her arms around me, she was repulsive, she pressed her face against mine, she was repulsive, and she stroked my bare shoulder, she was repulsive, and I repulsed, I began to stroke her neck, the back of her head, I massaged her scalp to calm her, and when she kissed my hair, grinding her groin against my thigh, I tore myself away, we looked at each other, gasping for breath, I was the more dazed of the two, she sober in a flash, one more enemy, tell your husband to see the lawyer tomorrow – it's going to be tomorrow, dear heart, tomorrow's the big day – and then when my husband came back (when he left he cast worried glances at his briefcase, would it hold all that money, because he had no idea how much *paper* it would be) and stood in the doorway, one look at him was enough, the way he hung his arm, like a penguin's wing, to know it had been called off, they had backed down, just like that, after a whole month. and my husband couldn't take it, he called the woman, and when he gave his name and she said what is it, what do you want, this gentle man began screaming, or nearly screaming, because he didn't know what he ought to be screaming, he just stammered, really, this won't do, it's not right, you can't do this, it's just not right, no, and why? and there was a pause, and my husband asked again, softly this time, why did this happen? and the answer was very interesting – my husband, after all, is a sucker for sentences like this – because, the woman said, *sir, it is a whole new ballgame now*, and my husband mumbled, ballgame? new? sir? what ballgame? and how new? and what sir? and then he heard a man's voice in the background, a voice to chill your blood, hang up already, you fuckin' bitch! and the woman hung up right away.

My precious gets cold feet faster than me, I guess. I'm listening to him once, he's reading something up on stage, faithful wife in the audience, when a cleanshaven, suntanned, athletic looking man settles down next to me, listen, Annika, I say to myself, if this man is not ÁVÓ then I am, and I am not, and he starts whispering about how tonight, later, the three of us, we'll have a nice chat, why are you whispering? I whisper, I just am, he whispers, besides, honey, the *body of the text* should be familiar to you by now, his name is written on his lapel, Ferenc, Ferenc, don't honey me if you don't mind, he glares into my face, probing the depths, we've already made plans for tonight, I whisper, oh, that's too bad! he whispers, when it would have been such an honour, with your husband, such an important representative of our cultural life, fuck off! enough already, look, dear Ferenc, dictatorship of the proletariat notwithstanding, my husband needs a woman tonight, understand? have a little consideration, it's not easy for me, either, you see, and I jumped up so my hair tickled his face as I brushed past, up on stage the reader paused, annoyed, this would cost me plenty, I ran outside to the ladies' room and leaned, heaving, against the tile and threw up, threaten and ingratiate, we'll find time for a little chat yet, don't you fear, and me pretending to be too obtuse, not that I was fooling anyone, though it's bound to happen if things keep up, and then my pet, his feelings still hurt, scolds and rebukes me, how I shouldn't fool around with them, preaching like my father-in-law used to, like one *who knows what he is talking about*, this is no game, you can play the hero here just so long, that's what makes this a landscape that is different, more barren and wild, more desolate and bleak, more brutal, because there's got to be some *little* order to life that no one should be allowed to upset, but these men have free access everywhere, they can make mincemeat of whatever takes their fancy, and there could be situations in which there is nothing you can bring up in your own defence, for no one's accusing you, there is no inner freedom and independence, only dependence and helplessness, because there is no place to hide, a barren, desolate wasteland, a country made of glass, they might be shadowing you, and then again they might not, there are no answers, for questions are not possible, that is the kind of place this is, you're sitting in a desolate spot on the edge of a forest, swallowing your tears, a citizen with full voting rights.

This is no deb's delight, but it's even worse when he is not scared, when if he so much as looks at a cop it's an extra two hundred, that's the way he looks, though he's as gentle as a lamb, the authorities can *read* him, an open book, if we get off with just two hundred we're lucky, my brother-in-law is a practical man, knows how to comply if it's in his interest, my husband in the car, his younger brother outside on the pavement, let's talk it over, nodding, bending over backwards, four hundred, three hundred, a hundred, it costs him nothing, he's even enjoying it, but of course, officers, oh yes, and my husband, he looks on, watches those Wicked Powers That Be take that big blockhead of a brother of his for a marionette, until enough! and he sallies forth, a Parsifal, searching for and finding wider relationships, about whose who is who and what should be done about it, and that they are supposed to be the brave guardians of his peace, are they not, civil courage, constitutionally, while the brave guardians listened, saluted, and left and proceeded to report my brother-in-law, who later turned up with the ticket, would my husband kindly pay the seven hundred forints, the price of his freedom, and was it worth it, but didn't stay for the answer, his brother soon bores him, that's the way it is, the one still talking while the other starts up the ignition.

The car's wheels were already in drive, too, when by way of an answer, the older of the two brothers cockily said it's no use worrying about questions of life and death, while I just grinned, a twentieth-century Virgin Mary (coloured lithograph). The question that my brother-in-law had posed in his unsparing and rather blatant manner was: what are we planning to do, should I, to put it bluntly, in spite of everything, get knocked up again.

Now I am really scared, possibly for the first time in my life.

I had to win my brother-in-law's acceptance, too; I can't say with much success. Here, it was an uphill fight for everything. You know, Bohumil, as I look at your family photographs, your father Frantzin, Uncle Pepin, I see the brewery, too, and I think I understand your mother perfectly. I also had to win the house over to my side; I was apprehensive, feeling I'd betrayed that other, the smaller one, abandoned it, cheated on it, passed it off.

I had more difficulty with the house just as my husband had less; he grew up here, and after we'd fixed up the attic the house changed, but it was *that old house* that changed, new paths appeared, unexpected spaces, unlooked-for silences, getting around became different too, new nooks and crannies took shape, and of the old, peaceful little hideaways it now turned out that there was always *somebody* there (it's a big family), the archetypal it is a yes only if it is a no situation, like with that goulash, the *trompe d'oeil* of past and present; after all, even my pet is that former child and he is not, the one groping in the dark now, terrified, for the former light switch on the barren wall.

Renovating the house was the first time, and pretty stormy at that, that my brother-in-law and family had to acknowledge my existence. I was as remote from their thoughts till then as Ushti nad Labem is from Jerusalem; they could take me or leave me, the choice was theirs to make. These people don't like it (and that included my precious), they don't appreciate the fact that there are *others* besides themselves; they have managed to accept themselves, an open-minded family if ever there was one, but they reserve their open-mindedness for themselves . . . Ever since we've lived here, my brothers-in-law never tire of telling us what *babes in the woods* they were, what innocents, letting themselves be conned into this switching of houses (hustling them out *de facto*, while also paying them off, as it were), that for our sake they passed off this veritable *Tuscan villa* for a song, letting it go to the dogs; while they, they were disinherited, so to speak, having yielded to the unspoken right of primogeniture on behalf of the eldest son; they pretended they were only joking, as if they were just testing me, and I good for a joke, even if it's at my own expense, when in point of fact they wanted me to hear their very real reproaches, to arouse a feeling of guilt, or a modicum of gratitude, at least – in me, and not in their brother, their own flesh and blood. I won't pretend, Bohush, that from time to time I'm not fed up with them.

Dear heart. Sometimes that's what I call him. But surely you (or he?) must tend a large garden, planting and replanting, like the Good Lord. And still I did not go to the doctor.

Renovating the house brought a slew of new experiences; we found ourselves entangled in novel, unfamiliar relationships, grown-up relationships, and I won't pretend that we were always on top of the situation. It took time to learn how to deal with these serious men. A carpenter or a mason is a very serious man. The mason and his team were already sitting in the garden half an hour before they started work, they had breakfast together, the mason sliced the bread and handed it out, like the head of the family to his children. That was authority, and we'd better learn to recognize it. And we couldn't get over what a lot of beer they drank. But with the plumbers and heating installers we learned that the masons did not drink a *lot* of beer. They drank nothing *but* beer. Which made them very reliable. We also learned in no time that authority and brains will not suffice for these dealings, the ability to have an overall view, cleverness, quick-wittedness, all go for nothing (virtues that my husband, after some legwork, was able to parade in front of the builders); it is *experience* that is needed, to wit, linguistic know-how. And this came as a surprise.

The road a *mittel-europeer* must traverse when negotiating with builders – for this clearly applies from Prague to Belgrade (and is a skill, in fact, that should come in especially handy at the GUM department store in Moscow) – this road runs parallel, if you'll excuse me, Bohumil, with Wittgenstein's; the elegant and rigorous geometric viewpoint is superseded by an approach more suited to the occasion, a more responsive, warmer, more personal touch. For instance, my husband thought at first that when he was quoted a price, it was what it was because that's what the price was, that's how much the thing was *worth*, less would make them suckers, more would be dishonest; he had no idea that the price first quoted means *nothing*, at most it is a friendly sign that there will eventually be *something*, some work done, and some payment, too, but let's not worry about it right now. During

the first month, still on this side of speech, my husband said
nothing, and paid through the nose. During the last month, by
then beyond it all, this same speechlessness was meta-
morphosed into an enchanting dialogue, a fencing match, a
dance of magnanimity and a dance of baseness, of power and
of weakness, a dialogue conducted by two people – two
men! – discussing the world, or rather, listening, listening to
what the world had to say . . . about itself. Reaching
an understanding was greatly facilitated at last by the fact
that in the meantime we had run out of money.

And energy. Don't think unkindly of him, Bohumil, but
he'd never done any physical work in his life. You didn't
become what you are just like that either. Though who knows
. . . So my precious learned to tote large bags of cement, at
first cuddling them in his lap, carefully, lovingly, like a novice
parent a sleeping child, in continual fear of the paper bag
ripping open and the fine, grey powder drizzling out for all
eternity; with time, though, he watched how the others do it,
how you had to go under it with one shoulder, shrugging it off
with the other as if to let the bag propel you forward.

But later, only the exhaustion remained, the early morning
awakenings, the constant state of readiness, the everydays of a
country that is not functioning. 'There is dust on my notepad!'
roared my precious, one fine day. For some reason, he had
started to hate me, too, by then. Who knows why. Actually,
I know. I know perfectly well. If he wants me to know
something, and not know it, he usually tells me at night, in my
sleep. I have dreamt about you often, Bohumil, so *you* must
know how sometimes one can't sleep, how one tosses and
turns and signs, and hoping against hope, do not open your
eyes.

But he just talked on and on about how you build a house
for yourself, fine, a house, a home, a refuge, fine, mothers,

matrons, feminine energies, fine, but *you*, this whole damn construction business just turns you on sexually, as you wipe off the old tables . . . your energy flowing into the handles you grab . . . and the increments, you can see it growing brick by brick, you made it grow out of your body, I know, with blood and sweat, each corner familiar, the corners of triumph and compromise, and you caress the freshly whitewashed walls with pride. He fell silent. I am always surprised to see him *composing* like that, even when he is alone, or thinks he is alone.

When he got to his knees I panicked, I stiffened my muscles; naked, he got to his knees, shouting, I'm just a helping hand around here, I know . . . that's why you leave me to fend for myself . . . but I refuse to be jealous of doorjambs and cross-beams . . . they satisfy you, I can tell . . . your body doesn't need, your body doesn't need me, and I refuse to accept that – but by then he was shaking me vehemently, while I, it's so ridiculous, really, pretended to be still asleep, as if I were in a dead faint in a man's arms, my head, my arms, flailing all over the place, I pretended I was having a bad dream, like someone raped in her sleep, that's what I did, Bohush, love, I felt nothing, because I really did have to try and sleep so that at dawn the next day I could be out at the Brickworks, in Solymár, and I did fall asleep without difficulty.

The days came and went, and it's just as well that it happened this way because with the help of a couple of brawny men you can move into a place in a single day, but to make a place lived-in takes time, time till you tame the house to your needs, till the objects find their proper places – that slow and lovely wandering, like a natural miracle – to feel at home. (At the high school reunion – the twentieth – the teacher [Sir!] remembered that my husband had lived here back then, too, and said, smiling, 'Aha! In which case, you're likely to die there as well.' My husband had no ready answer, so he smiled back.)

Dear heart, I'm in a rotten mood. Though you mustn't think it's infidelity.

Pussy blues, that's what it is. I don't want any more children. As far as wanting goes, I did not want anything up till now either; my children, too, I did not *want*, after all, there was never any question of me *not* wanting them, while *sober* reflection will never result in children; bringing children into the world in this place is, to say the least, not logical.

I don't want to. I don't want to. I don't want to. I don't want to push my big stomach in front of me, I don't want to wear the same old dress for six months on end, I don't want to stuff iron capsules down my throat, I don't want to vomit, I don't want to hurt, I don't want the hospital, I don't want smiling strangers groping my insides, I'm worried about my breasts, I don't want them to swell up, and I don't want them to sag. – Bohumil, old friend! You won't believe what I saw the other day! An old woman up on the women's sundeck, but with perfect schoolgirl breasts, I just gawked, they were so delicious, I thought – until their owner laughed sternly at me! – and I don't want to change diapers, I don't want to be up to my elbows in shit, and I don't want to be any more beautiful either, I don't want to start all over again, I want no new joys, the old will more than suffice, thank you, it's all I can do keeping up with them.

My body, dear heart, is as reliable as clockwork, that's why there has never been any fear in me. Now there is. That's what I mean when I say I'm in trouble now. That's why there's trouble ahead.

I have a story about a swan, my husband says, I'll let him have it (meaning *you*), takes nerve, don't you think? 'Somewhere in Germany, in a town by the side of a lake, a flaming swan flew into the evening sky night after night, *divne ptak*, and when it had burned up, it plunged into the lake; the citizens were horrified, they posted guards and caught a young man red-handed as he lured another swan with a bit of croissant, drenched it with a bottle of gasoline, then set it on fire, and looked on bewitched as the swan flew into the night . . . and when he was caught, this young man said in his defence that the inspiration came from Salvador Dali, that the nightmare vision of the burning giraffe that Dali had painted haunted him at night so that the room in which he dreams about the burning giraffe and Salvador Dali's paranoid-critical method began to hurt, first he tried to drench the giraffe and its mane at the zoo but could not reach up that high, and so coaxed a gentle swan to come to him instead, and when the swan took off in flames, all the way up, at the zenith, he saw Salvador Dali's burning giraffe . . . and the world did not hurt him after that, and he didn't know that this picture would upset me as much as the mirror of the fishpond was upset by that gorgeous swan as it plummeted into the cooling water . . .'

I have a secret for you. It's not pressing yet. You can't know who Mano Kogutowicz is; a map-maker, among other things, the map-maker of a country that existed once. Your country, the present one, the one that was *made*, and mine, too – these are just barely there, they're there and they're not.

Sitting on a bench in the Inner City – I was out of breath – an old woman settled next to me, I seem to attract them, there are always a number of them around me, and she shows me Vörösmarty Square, and Váci utca, see what they've done to this city, a Potemkin village at best, a false front, but believe you me, Budapest was a fabulous city once, a great place to live in, dear, I loved strolling down its streets, I loved shopping, looking, because you were pleased to be young back then, mam, *pleased*, that I was, but that's not the point, it was a real city, with real people, like Paris or Berlin.

For you, Bohoushek, Prague is a real city, I can see that. For me, Budapest is not. But I will try to conjure up Manó Kogutowicz's colours . . . I will be that old woman on the bench for you, I will grow old to suit you, your backache no longer anything to worry about. You shouldn't put your hopes up; besides, far as I'm concerned, your bearing is *stately*. I will convince you that we have an ocean. I will expand the width of the Danube, it's my elemental duty. We will sit on the shore of this ocean of Budapest. Budapest is situated along the shore of the ocean named after her, a fisherman's paradise renowned for its crayfish, which the Hungarians call *goulash*. We'd eat crayfish there with light but cold white wines, though sometimes we'd eat stew and something or other with semolina dumplings, *reprove*, *knedlík*, *zeli*, God forbid people should think we're devoid of the proper national sentiment. The essence of the ocean is that it is always different. Different from the shore, and different from a boat. And different when you're alone, and different, again, when you're looking at it in company.

'Dinner is served.' (Victor Hugo)

I'd show you around, what do you say? wine you and dine you, and show you the world. Bohoushek! I've got it! I'd *keep* you! A gigolo in your old age. How about it? And don't tell me the thought has never crossed your mind . . . You'd send me the bills, and I'd pay through the nose . . . Beer, books, champagne, women, no, I take that back, I'd scratch out all of your ten eyes, what I mean is, the other way around, your two eyes with my ten claws, but a jacket, that I'd buy you, under the counter, an ancient tweed, of course, and one of those modern light ones, we'd turn up the sleeves, we'd get it for a song . . .

You'd be deeply touched. And you'd want to protect me. Take my father's place. I could always use a calm, resigned, Czech dad . . . Apparently, Philip Roth's mother always wanted to say, my son, the doctor; and me, I want to say, my father, the *Czech* – as for my husband, if we're not too choosy we could round him up a stray mom, he's not particular – and that's that.

Or is that what is considered 'too much of a good thing'? (Have you ever wondered about where *sweetness* is lodged? In what it is contained? Or am I insatiable? Aunt Georgina asked me once, as if she were asking are you tired? do you speak German? – are you insatiable? Are you insatiable, Bohumil?)

I'd put my arm through yours and from time to time, squeeze your elbow ever so gently. You wouldn't bat an eye, yet you would *pre-sent-ly* squeeze me back. This is how we'd talk until our throats dried out. I'd show you Hungary. But possibly the whole world. Or just one room. Be it as it may, one thing I know: you and I, the two of us together, we could make the Danube Confederation of States a reality. How all those simpletons would gawk! Would they be against it back in your country? My husband would never notice; he'd be tickled pink that the problem of the small nations had been solved.

We'd be there, just that, no more, just be there, there in Prague and there in Budapest, flying hither and thither, you'd get sick on the plane all the time, your palms sweating, and talk nonsense, not a pleasant thing to behold, frightened out of your pants, leaning your brow on my shoulder, a youthful, female shoulder, after all! and I'd take your trembling, blotched hand, and from this and the wrinkles on your face, conjure up your writings, all those remarkable *multitudes* of people, *your* people, those unforgettable Czech characters . . . A novelist is a story-teller, after all! And as such, a favourite of the gods.

Our presence wouldn't be like the light but more like a veil, a soft, drizzling, mildly unfriendly rain, in which the cities would shine forth without losing their drummed-in, well-earned gloom. The mere savouring of the meaninglessness of our journey fills us with bitterness, and beauty. (You said it.)

Our being there would inspire others to *be* there as well. Just think, Bohush, how frenetic that would be! Everyone that is would *be*! Oh, would that be a how-dee-do! Nowhere to hide, except behind your own tattered fate, nothing you could really call hiding at all.

All this would happen gradually, like the universal triumph of socialism, first the objects, then the dogs, cats, pigeons, swans, and last but not least, man himself. For instance, the bridges would get all mixed up, a confused situation would develop, but we wouldn't force the Danube under Charles Bridge, we wouldn't go that far, it would only scare people off, the Danube, for this purpose, is too big, but the ocean I've created from it to please you, the ocean, the Ocean of Budapest, would serve the purpose, it wouldn't be too big; being infinite, it's flowing along behind our house.

We're river people, you and I. Could this ocean be the ocean of infidelity? The gauge of defeat? What is the trap we are walking into *now*?

(– because he takes everybody apart, because that's what he's like, he takes everybody he loves apart, then is surprised, surprised like a child, when sometimes he can't put them back together again.)

So then. Tomorrow I'm having this baby aborted. Think of me at the stroke of midnight, not that anything is bound to happen then, nothing is going to happen then, except that you will be thinking of me.

Guess what. I'm being tailed. They're nuts. I've never had illusions, never chased after socialist mirages, so to speak, but this is too much, you'd think idiocy had its limits, like anything else.

Once – once upon a time, and a long time ago it was, when the revolution was still referred to as a counter-revolution and the massacre was called tragic, and (in the spirit of self-criticism) the looting of a nation a mistake, the murderers were judged but were not called to account, after the red, white, brown and multi-coloured terrors, this grey terror, which was called the subterranean spring of reform-communism, flowed along peacefully, comparatively speaking, there was less catharsis to the stories, no one was hanged, and no one was quartered, in accordance with orders from Moscow, it was said, people's lives were not ruined outright the way it happened thirty, forty years before, history did not wreak havoc with its cast of characters so they'd end up sitting alone by the side of an unfamiliar ditch, the only tangible thing still part of their lives being the side of the ditch itself, no, lives were not turned topsy-turvy this time around, lives were just . . . bent out of shape, they began to droop. Lives wilted.

In short, samizdat was still samizdat, and the one-party

system the guarantee of future development, when once, I kid you not, the democratic police caught me red-handed. I had bought a sack of potatoes, and pulled up in front of the house (where those guys are now standing with their Lada), when, just like in a Yankee flick in living colour, three police cars, sirens blaring, blue light flashing, appeared from behind the bushes and surrounded me. (We gotcha covered!) Questions, answers, petty impertinences, the way they quickly realized they'd put their foot in it – Comrades, you have put your foot in my mouth! I was at the ideal Balzacian age then – cross my heart and hope to die, you know what they said? they said in the future I'd better keep my Trabant clean, it's an eyesore on the urban landscape! How right you are, said I, that's the Trabant for you, an eyesore on the urban landscape.

A young man who wrote samizdat lived near us, that's what confused them. I saw him on TV the other day, keeping his mouth politely buttoned up as the ruling party's impeccably sweatered representative assured him of his good will and told him of his conviction, to wit, that the service the young man had rendered during the past ten years was impressive, and isn't it a regrettable paradox that it had to be him of all people whose job it was to suppress it. We're living in an age of transition, the reporter said. – Bohush! Have you ever lived in an age that was not in transition?

Once before, in another age of transition, I have already cried over you, my dear. 'In early 1975 Hrabal gave an interview which was not so much self-criticism as a hastily delivered declaration of allegiance to the otherwise unspecified, most recent resolution of the most recent party congress. As Karel Kyncl, who at the time was still living there, tells it, in their bitter disappointment the youth of Prague reacted by publicly burning the books of their idol, Hrabal, on Kampa, a picturesque isle on the Moldva.' My first child was born that year. You were on my mind a lot, then. And how I loathed those smart-ass culture hounds, those body snatchers . . . That's when I sent you, old friend, a pebble, it was from Rhodes, there was a white line running around it, a rarity . . . I also glued a white elephant to it, you know, Rilke's white elephant . . . *Nehci, abys na to odpovídal*).

Their car's been hanging around for days. I first spotted them around the time I told my husband about the new child. They've been tailing me ever since, I can tell. Two young men. One, in fact, one of them, is younger than the other, may the green-eyed monster consume you, Bohumil Hrabal! They're giving me the eye, the once-over; they bombard me with tokens of their respect.

I got up early this morning. I do not like to get up early, and I do not make a habit of it. My mother and mother-in-law, they used to get up at five-thirty, and by seven everything stood ready, the table laid, the food steaming . . . This too has passed. My children think that breakfast – in Europe, at least – is a custom exclusive to Saturday and Sunday, a form of feasting reserved for weekends.

I spotted them right away, they were sleeping in the Lada, arms and legs akimbo; I snuck up to them, they were beautiful, except . . . they were men! With stubble. At night, as we slept inside, all *unsuspecting*, they grew a beard. I found this touching. Poor darlings, growing all over the place while they sleep. Their hair and nails, too, I guess. I look at their nails. They don't bother with the nails these days, I think. But they still *nail* you. And when they do, a slap in the face is still a slap in the face. Yes, they must slap you instead these days. Thrash you. Beat you to a pulp. They're beating men, *homo beating*. The lips of the older one droop as if he were pulling on

106

them, as if he were on the verge of tears, a pencil sketch for a cry, a weathered man's face, handsome, same age as Christ.

They're such cute cowards, though, wanting to stop and talk to me more than once, I could tell. Especially the younger of the two. But he just hems and haws, gawks like a turkey. Maybe he's a deaf-mute.

Tell me, love of my life, Bohumil – honest, Bohumil, if it weren't for you I'd be all out of Bohumils – I'd happen to be walking with you here, on the shore of the Budapest Ocean, me barefoot in the sand, you, bowing to your social prestige, in a serious, seriously tattered pair of sneakers, there'd be a bench in the lukewarm wind, we'd sit down and jump up, you'd feel yourself too old for me again (though that would be the least of it), and I'd be very angry, besides, for me it's no big deal to be of the same age; anyway, tell me, my only one: in your opinion, does the ÁVÓ employ deaf-mutes?

At which you'd say, pussywillows, there's no ÁVÓ any more, you should know that, because you'd be a real *expert* on the former secret police (what did you call them back home?), and without further ado, would start into a story there on the Duna Corso where we'd be strolling, about the Solovki camp or whatever, but more specifically, about one of its guards, who specialized in gold teeth, picking them out and having them shot, enhancing his collection, busy as a bee, but then the whatchamacallit of socialist justice caught up with him for purposes of retribution, and he got ten years, of which he did twelve, twelve days, and so on and so forth, because you're a veritable treasure-trove of stories, there's not a story you don't know, and the stories know you, too, they want to be admitted to your presence at the first possible opportunity, trekking on and on in the forest of Kersko in the direction of your small cottage, patiently waiting if you're not home, feeding the cats, too, Latvian, Polish, Slovene, Romanian, Ruthenian stories, you'd be telling me these on the seashore, a stone's throw from Elizabeth Bridge, and right away they'd turn into Hungarian and Czech stories, of course, because of us, the way you hold my arm, and sometimes the back of your hand would press against my ribcage, they always were, they're all the same story, only the adjectives differ, the colours, the passion, but the suffering is the same, the nakedness, they're itinerant stories, in a village they gathered together all the homing pigeons, promised that not so much as a hair would be hurt on anybody's head, then they stopped on the five hills surrounding the village, tied tiny live torches to the pigeons, each a live match, then set them free, go home! and they stood on the hilltops until everything had burnt to the ground, this is a Russian story, and that there was this gifted boy, a violinist, who stood behind the gate and knew that it was just a matter of seconds and the tanks would flatten everything level with the ground, and he began playing his violin, and he had to be dragged from there days later, gone in the head and aged, his face shrivelled up, that's a Hungarian story, but enough! and I'd lift your blotched hand to my cheek.

But this would embarrass you. Whether they use deaf-mutes now, my dear, I do not know. If the deaf-mute is eminently qualified – your eyes would be searching for some beer, you'd laugh out loud: I suppose so. They can always use men who are as silent as the grave.

(Silent as the grave. Since 1989, this has no meaning in Hungarian any more. The graves are doing so much talking, it's all one can do, just keeping up.) (I just read the 'official version of the '56 shooting meant for revenge and intimidation': forty thousand prince-primates, princes, counts and barons who, due to their class origins, camouflaged themselves as foundry men from Red Csepel, and with bread under their arms, took it into their heads to attack the peacefully sniping ÁVÓ men.)

My husband had a schoolmate, his mind like a fire-cracker he was so bright, and looked like the writer Kálmán Mikszáth, too; he used to point all the time, he had puffy, round hands with fingers like miniature sausages, yet his hands fluttered every which way, everything about him awkward and crude – the movement of his hands, his eyes and his brains; they were the exception. All his ancestors worked on the soil, or to resort to Marxist jargon, the thirst for knowledge had accumulated in him through the centuries, he was a pig for knowledge, and when in college during his first lecture the professor did not speak about district regulations and our compulsory class outing but said instead: Good morning, colleagues, let us consider the 'A' mass – a silent elation shook this eighteen-year-old man to the core, knowing he'd come to the right place, in a month he was called in to police headquarters, and from then on, for five years, every week there were these small slips of paper waiting for him, *greetings from your mathematician friend Gyuri*, in bars and cafés, later they'd sit in cars, circling in the city, in out-of-the-way districts, then even at night, in silence, for hours, and then they went out to a plough-land and stopped on a dirt road and waited and said nothing, who're we waiting for? and they waited and said nothing, who're we waiting for? with the ignition on, the boy sitting with three grown men, all mute, for you, Laci, they were on first-name basis by then, for you, Laci, to come to your senses, and they took him home and dropped him at the door, very proper like; from time to time Major Jascsák would come down from Pest to co-ordinate – at which time everybody shit in their pants, until finally he had to sign a paper that what he knows, not that he knows anything, is a state secret, it's gonna cost him five years unless he's as silent as the grave, my signature might still be there, filed in the archives, God, how many similar slips! the sixties and seventies, to which they like to refer now as the time of unpretentious material gain, idyllic, were for me the years of fear, I was a child, I knew nothing, let's look at the 'A' mass, that's what I knew, that's what I wanted to know, I wasn't a coward but I had no idea what was what, I had no idea what meant what and to what point, how many times I'd planned to jump on top of the table in the student cafeteria and say it and say it and scream into their mugs until the entire student body started vomiting, I was a child, and they scared me, but he was not scared for life, he outgrew it, his eyes as bright as ever, like the eyes of an old, sly gypsy woman who is inexplicably also a prince, over-refined, the refinement of centuries in him, the heaviness of the soil and the refinement of collective wisdom, and when he goes to his lecture, he says good morning, colleagues, let us consider the 'A' mass.

You can hardly breathe, everything is so stuffy here. Which is enough to put you in a bad mood, but it's not the bad mood that's the worst. – Do you know whom I used to exchange letters with regularly about the weather? My mother-in-law's mother, and in English, to further my education. There was nothing I did not know then about the meteorological misery of Transdanubia. We showed the correspondence to an English friend of ours, who became ever so excited about the perfection with which my husband's grandmother had mastered the English language; for instance, I find it very hard to believe, but there are supposed to be expressions in English you must not use, not only in speech, but in a letter, it's just not done, except on an *open* postcard, and apparently, grandma never slipped up. English is a refined language. Hungarian is wonderful, it's fine, but it is not refined. Here there is no – or almost no – instance of 'it's just not done'. Or it's not proper. Or not salutary. Here, anyone may be gifted. To prod a ballet dancer into an argument in a highly dubious fashion by resorting to the frequentative mode: that's what an English verb is like – according to its defamators.

By the way, our English friend always brings flowers. Now that is something you can build a world empire on . . .

Ridiculous. But you. Why aren't you here, around the corner, instead of out there in the sticks? You're too close and you're too far. Around the corner, that's where your place is. I know you know: I'm taking advantage of you, I'm holding on. You're my 'man for all seasons'.

Were I to receive a letter from you, I wouldn't open it right away. Caution first, pleasure after. Take it by degrees, let the excitement mount. I'd hide the letter, not from my husband, though I may not show it to him, I'd hide it from myself, from my curiosity, which is non-personal, and would therefore offend you. The day would pass with this hiding, and by degrees I'd become ripe for your letter. I'd prepare myself, adapt. I'd make dinner, send the kids to bed with a Judas-kiss, hide in a remote corner of the house; your words, cocky news, obviously, wouldn't matter any more – compared to the day that had passed.

Once I'd like to explain to you how Spanish women make love. It would have no actuality, but would add to your knowledge. The Spanish woman is strong and humble. If you're out walking with me, you needn't pretend you're younger than your years. Pant all you want. Feel how tired you are! After a good bout of love-making, the Spanish woman always says she's tired. That I'm tired, and she stretches her limbs. So keep that in mind.

I had a beautiful dream last night, I dreamt a beautiful word, the word 'mondsee'. Mondsee-blues. *Ach, wissen Sie* – I always wanted to start a letter this way.

But of that not a word. Of that not a word all day and all night, of that not a word twenty-four hours of the day, in the morning, when the kids have left for school, and it's just the two of us, in the grey, freezing-cold kitchen, both of us dull with sleep, worn to a frazzle, I of this *thing*, and he of you, Bohumil – I can't stand it, I can't stand it, he cries in his room from time to time when he knows I can't hear, or rather, when he knows I can just barely hear, or that I might be thinking that he might be thinking that I can't hear, this is the extent of his prudery, clear and transparent like a mountain stream; he really let you have it, he was up till two, we don't look each other in the eye and blame you for everything, dear, we possibly can, on 'that Czech pig, that Svejk-offspring, that *knedli*-glutton, that beer-barrel, last night I sat for two hours without a word, just staring into the dark, I didn't work, I didn't read, I didn't think, I didn't fantasize, I just sat with *that man's* book in my lap, the one with the brewery and the cutting off of hair, and I didn't want anything, not even for the knowledge to seep into me directly, there into my lap, not even that, just for time to pass and for me to get drowsy so I could go to bed at last, so I wouldn't have to do anything any more'; when speaking of things to do (the everyday life of a family-factory), of that we say nothing to our children, calling them to account in voices sharper than usual, what do you think this is, a hotel or something, etc., our idiocy growing by leaps and bounds, by now we don't even feel like talking with each other, and if we do, it's generally the sending of messages back and forth, one of the most widespread of parental vulgarisms, via the children.

An ounce of prevention, they say, is worth a pound of cure. Well, I've despaired of the prevention and despaired of the cure. I'm scared and I'm alarmed. A brand new experience. We've been living a lie for days; I don't lie, the day lies, the time, the space, the air, my every breath, the slit between two eye-lashes, the space between my legs, too, is a lie, even my honesty is a lie. And it's because we're living under the jurisdiction of an even greater lie.

The Prince of Falsehood hath entered all our halls, uninvited, his numerous retinue in train, extending a semi-gracious reception, everybody who is anybody is there, *tout Paris* . . .

Our thinking putrefied in no time at all; I wouldn't have believed it if I hadn't seen it with my own eyes.

The misgiving came from within, just as the certainty had before. My body is not reaching me, it's not calm: so what's going on? What's the picture? I don't know. Not my soul, not my morals, not my self – my body, it's my body that has failed me, it won't speak to me. With the other babies every bone in my body was joyous, delirious. My room was brighter. The price of meat dropped. On the street, people turned their heads, the women whispering enviously, the men sighing hopelessly, the buses re-routed, floods in South America and drought in India – you understand, Bohumil, the world changed, the CIA turned into a literary society and irrefutable evidence of the existence of God was found in Baku. Now I shiver, I have goosebumps all day, I'm goosebumping, and I'm getting pimples, and I can feel the birth pangs all over again, no, no, no, and when I touched my breast under the shower, and couldn't feel anything, because it was like I'd suffered frost-bite, indifferent, I started to cry, I didn't want this, nobody wanted this, who wanted this? so then, why . . . The thing I was perhaps most intimate with turned against me, my own body. My traitorous body, forsake me not.

It is a fact that 'hrabal' means 'to scrape'? (I refuse to think it through to its logical conclusion.) (I scrape after you, cutie-pie, I am about to be scraped, I am a virgin girl at her scraping, a scrapee, scraped bacon rind.)

I've tried a hot bath and I've tried rum; in secret, we haven't lied to each other openly yet, this too took time to develop. – I shouldn't go into details, but I will, Bohumil, you do the same, Health Service doc, up on table, legs apart, Health Service doc shakes hands with child to be, a Dutch test disk, congratulations, mom.

My little chickadee, too, playing the innocent for all he's worth, hoping I'll find a way, without his help, let us hope. Time flows by . . . where? where?

When I said in so many words what scared me, it was terrible. It was terribly *small*. And went against the very thing I was anxious about. Because there is something I fear from this new baby, I fear that he'll be taking instead of giving. I say it is terrible, but there you have it, I've said it. We are helpless, and this has never happened to us before (yes, I know, it's

114

ludicrous); there are only bad choices to be made, if I choose this, it's bad, and if I choose that, that is bad as well, and no other choice in sight; I am choosing this, and this is going to make it just too much, it's been too much as is, much that was difficult, and good, and that sneak-thief, time, is at our heels, too, catching up, just as it catches up with everyone, I know! I'm about to give in, give in to something I would not have accepted before, I'm not saying Bohumil, that I haven't given up anything before, I give up something every second of the day; *at one time* even your mother cut off her ale-coloured hair, and I can also tell that my life is slowing down, and speeding up, making an about-face, and often not as I would have wished – but I have not suffered defeat, or what is less, but more important, I would not accept it for what it was, defeat is the only payoff, it's what I was afraid of, the defeat, but if I choose that, that other choice, what will happen later, if I should happen to wake up in the middle of the night two years from now, let's say, what am I to say then? what am I to say and to whom? who will I make my excuses to and in what way? who will I hate? and will there be anyone who shall escape my hatred?

My nose started bleeding: I woke up to what our King Attila had not: I was surprised, I couldn't budge for some time, my whole face covered with blood, my neck, my nightie, the douvet soaked through, the blood sticky, slippery, then I got up, held a handkerchief to my nose, threw back my head, ridiculous, this proud posture in the middle of all the muck, the blood wouldn't stop flowing, down the hall, in a narrow stream, then down the stairs, that's what woke me, the blood from my nose prancing down the stairs. Could it have been a wish for the baby to abort through the nose?

No problem. I'll speak to the reverend father, I thought. But what's the use, I know what he's going to say. What he knows I know. Or should I go and admire the clever way sympathy and severity dovetail through his soft-spoken words? No thank you! Let *him* have this baby. Let the pontiffs have the babies. And I'll hold their cute little heads as they sweat.

Do you know what I would like, Bohumil? Nice and easy, without even thinking about it, to abort this baby, *just a little* . . . Everything, and I mean everything, feels as if it weren't really happening to me. That's why my conscience is clear. As if I were reading about it. (Or writing about it.) I'd like this baby to be slowly absorbed, transformed into a lovely simile at my husband's hands, a balloon, or the parliament . . .

Why? Why did you place such a burden on us? – Specialized knowledge is putrefied knowledge; only the whole makes any sense, there's no specialized consciousness, left-over brains, specialized rationalization; we are thinking exclusively now of what is in our interest; and in order to avoid cynicism, we have created complex structures of thought; wandering inside its bowels, we need not face the fact that the embryo is a human being. That was just by way of an example. I won't ask you, Bozo, what you . . . honest I won't. I promise: I will be thinking of you all the time. I must soon make up my mind. I have run out of excuses.

I have been praying in earnest for days. Like a summer shower, except badly, by rote. Yet pray I must. Praying does not solve anything by changing the world or turning on a light in our brain, but it makes an infinitesimal change in that numbness that makes everything seem unalterable, hopeless, and all this because a little something happens inside, radically inconsequential, no more, perhaps, than the awkward inclination for prayer.

Nothing happened. I attended Mass every morning, looking for silence and the suitable passages from the Holy Scriptures, despair not, o ye of little faith, etcetera, I hiked into the mountains, I sat atop cliffs, summits, I tried everything (except the ocean, the ocean I am keeping in reserve for you, my dear), everything that could steer me towards the infinite. I fasted. I refused him my body, though truth to tell, he did not ask for it, we lay in bed like brother and sister, anxious and apprehensive. I have made up my mind, Bohush. In my dream you were me, and I said to me, to you, or the other way around: why don't you please dream about *me*, for a change, you'll see, in your dream I will not be ungrateful. Tomorrow. So then, it is to be tomorrow.

Today is tomorrow. Tomorrow's night, a hard tomorrow's night, and what could have been left behind. Point by point, *nice* and proper, I will tell you what happened. Having a purpose in mind reduces fatigue but increases the consumption of alcohol. You wrote that, I swear. – Generally, I need to speak with you urgently about every five minutes, and this complicates my life. But what has been done cannot be undone. If only you were with me now. – If, if, iffity if . . . if the church steeple had a prick it'd be my grandad Dick, yes, and we'd take long walks, and you'd set me straight about the ways of the world . . .

Last night. The phone rings, I pick it up, nobody at the other end, I can hear the silence, he puts it down. Again. Does the car with such and such a licence plate belong to me? And he's Captain Kárász. Caress? No, Kárász, mam, and he laughs.

Sorry. So then, the two older children and my husband have suffered a fatal accident, a head-on collision. Whose fault? It's all I can get out, as if it mattered in some way. An infraction by a Soviet tank, says Captain Kárász, but I caution you, mam, not to regard it as politically inspired. Besides, I give you my word, they did not suffer, and he puts the receiver down. I went to the kitchen and spooned into the cold paprika-potato leftovers. My husband spoons into things that way, and I think it's appalling. Our youngest, the loquacious girl, was sleeping in the inner room with a high fever. I changed the compress on her wrists and ankles.

Once she slipped and scraped her knee, and started squealing like a stuck pig. It can't hurt that bad, stop bawling. It's not hurting at all. Then why are you bawling? Because my skin's been *damaged*. Everything that is not perfect pains her. She's the hardest to figure out because she does all the figuring. I like to see myself in her, filling her words with what I know, the way we grown-ups always do. Children are really innocent and wild. I can see the way she looks at my husband, like one who knows that she can wind this man around her little finger, and sometimes she takes advantage of it, sometimes not.

Her lips were chapped from the fever, she had trouble breathing, I bend over her, and without thinking, without any thoughts at all – I did not start to strangle her, I did strangle her. So I could be completely alone. *All* my relations must die. Everyone around me! So no one should remind me of that half-finished other . . . The phone rang, and I was glad because I knew I would not talk for years, I wouldn't say anything to anybody, I don't want to arouse sympathy with my words, nor new hatred, for that matter. I would remain silent. Except just the last phone call.

This is Kárász. Anna, is that you? I said nothing. I know

what you're thinking. At least we tried, tried to appear different than usual . . . Who knows, Anna, what kind of animal is hiding in us? It'd take a writer to answer that one, not a husband, Anna. – I waited some more, keeping the joy of speaking in reserve for later. Kárász changed his tune, you rotten whore. If you think confession helps, you've been hoodwinking yourself for the past twenty years!

I slammed down the phone. That instant, there was a ring at the door. I did not move. They banged on the door. Naked, I went to open it. Don't open it, came a muffled voice from outside. I recognized the voice, it was Captain Kárász, but I asked who it was anyway. Don't ask, it's better for you, too, if you don't know too much. And grab a robe, or you'll catch cold. What do you want? I wailed. In the name of the people, they'd say in a Hungarian film in colour, at this point they fell silent, I returned, at my bed a condor preening itself. In its eyes I saw my mother's never-ending disillusionment.

Yet I don't usually have such dreams. I drew no conclusions. But I felt irritated when in the morning I saw all those *many* living beings eat, chat, brush their teeth, go to the toilet, I looked at them but thought of you. Take care of yourself. If anything happens to you, I'm going to kill you. I intend to be a perennial plant in your garden. I need your surly temper.

The morning. We inherited Terike from my mother-in-law; my father-in-law impressed her, how is he? what a good-looking man! she used to say, she's a whiz at cleaning the house, I'm a little in awe of her, she always gets her way, she hates books, dust traps, she says, she hates each book separately, talks of them as if they were close relations, where are those three blasted Kosztolányis? (thinking of the volume of short stories), just a child, my little Celine (*Journey to the End of the Night*), come to mummy, and slaps them around as if she really knew something about Celine, two years ago she appeared with a lank, threadbare man, some extra help for the mistress, from now on old man Feri's going to do the work for me; since then it's been the two of them, Terike sits down, they drink three bottles of beer, buying them is my responsibility, and she bosses 'the old man' around, who despite this 'old' is a good ten years her junior; I left out a bottle of cognac once, and Terike got drunk, when I got home she said, you like *a good stake in your ground*, no doubt, mistress, careful you don't regret it; old man Feri finished cleaning up, eyes lowered, apologized, pulled that great hunk of a woman to her feet, Terike, my angel, it's time to go, and she let herself be dragged out the door, like a helpless imbecile.

Today I'm going to confide in you, mistress . . . actually, I'm taking you into my confidence, she said to me the minute I got back from shopping; the old man is gay, but you see, Annika, what a good man he is, quiet, doesn't drink, what else do you need? I haven't been with a man for twelve years, what's the use, I need it like a hole in the head, while the old man's a proper sort, he's got a boyfriend, real discreet, I understand; you know what having a man in my bed was like? pure hell, nothing but suffering, and me pregnant all the time, my husband had such damned hot balls may he rot in his grave; others put up with it too, he said, and I couldn't push him off either, his hairy body and prick sticking to you like glue, I used to scrape it out with a hairpin, then I got fed up and wouldn't let him, he said it'll kill him if he can't hide between my legs, it'll kill him, and a good thing, too, I said, go right ahead, and he did, but if it was from this or something else I wouldn't know, I didn't think much of him, couldn't care less, him taking his stake someplace else; I thought highly of him once, just once, the summer of '48, because he was a paratrooper officer, and the asshole parachuted out on top of the star over Parliament on St Stephen's day; I look up at that beautiful dome atop Parliament, go look, Teri, isn't that your husband there on top of Parliament, I really looked up to him then, just that once.

I can see the hairpins in the mind's eye, the variously shaped, new, old, rusty hair pins, all that blood, all the blood of all the women, the clots of blood, the mucus, the platelets with plasma, as they glide down the wide-open thighs, our stretched-out thighs, our crying, that no one wants to hear, the bodies gone bad, the scabs and scars, my sisters stabbed, struck-down, and me, the living dead. – This wasn't quite authentic either. As if I were thinking of somebody else, as if all this had nothing to do with me. I really did lose myself, I saw no one I could have pointed to, it's *you*! My husband says it's a waste of time, cleaning windows, a clean window is unnatural, while a so-called dirty window is organic, he's nuts.

The shopping. Today, when for the first time in my life I saw the milk dripping from the carefully selected bag of milk on to the carefully selected bread loaf, for the first time in my life, I started screaming in the store, flung all the stuff back on the shelves one by one, the ones in plastic bags twirled like a sling-slot, the ones in paper bags with a putting shot, then I ran out between the rows of my cheering audience.

In front of the grocery store, I met a real shaman from Lapland, a medicine woman, and she even sang her own *yoyk* (that's a medicine song, her forebears' family song) and the song of the wind. When we parted she took my hand, and I can still feel a surge of energy in my palm. A medicine woman like this could do so much with one's life, if only one would let her!

When I started towards the Lada, they started, too, I picked up speed, and so did they, more, more, I broke into a run, more. I stopped, they stopped. I panted. I didn't know what I wanted. I watched them from a distance. What would happen if I'd keep you as my only transgression? The older one, or maybe just more mature, made a face, like when someone's had enough of his whore. The little one, who is actually pretty tall, did as he had the other night: he raised his index finger to his lips. What should I not talk about? Or was he sending a kiss?

Of course, the sentence is addressed to you, Bohush, it's yours, but I have squandered it away. What would happen if I kept you as my only transgression?

The afternoon. I lowered my head, I walked as if against a strong wind, all I saw was the sidewalk. My sister-in-law made an appointment for me with her obstetrician, a decent, competent guy, you'll see. At the doctor's office I was greeted by an old man. I'm in trouble, I say to him, I'm pregnant. What?! Repeat that, will you? I repeat it. That's excellent, he says all starry-eyed. I wait. The first? no, Doctor, the fourth, it's butchers and obstetricians we use such gentle tones with, excellent, smiles the old man, giving me a merry once-over, *cap à pied*, congratulations, my dear! a fine thing! the first is always the best, dear, you'll see, it's like you're creating the world, you know, have you ever given birth, Doctor? naturally! naturally! he nods vehemently, I have four beautiful daughters! four! I'll prescribe some iron, DON'T! I scream, I want this baby done away with! he looked at me, all smiles, he shook his head as if talking to a mischievous child, all right, dear, all right, it doesn't have to be iron, you can eat apples instead, and never you mind what people say, a glass or two of red wine never hurt anybody, you'll see.

I walked out without even saying goodbye. F-f-f-f-f-fuck yoo-hoo a-a-a-all, I sobbed, leaning against the wall.

I'm thinking about you, Bohumil. Who are you? I won't go into detail.

Laughing, the assistant builders from next door whistled after me, *come-on-every-body, dooh-daah* . . . I turned round and gave them a look that made the rest get stuck in their throat. But one of them came over to me, right up close, opened his mouth, but nothing came out. Ah . . . ah . . . he groaned, and looked me deep in the eye. Wo . . . wo . . . workfo' . . . da-da lo-o-rd . . . kk . . . carrydem . . . bb . . . bricks . . . kk . . . calmly . . . yoo-hoo lov'lee . . . ff . . . freckle. I turned on my heels and left him standing there.

We have received the sign, and oh, what joy in our humble abode! The old, deaf doc, that's the sign. The one we've been waiting for. In which case it's all right. It's OK. We have been shown. Shown the way. The Word cited. We chased our present children out of the kitchen and opened a bottle of champagne. And drank it down. Pause. Now what? Champagne? Gone. In a funk, though not quite unexpectedly, I realized everything was starting all over again. Sign? What sign? The restlessness in my body, that's what sign! Oh my womb, sing unto me. Cunt dys-pho-nia, lap-a-pho-nia.

I had to get out of that kitchen, I did not want to look at the man sitting across from me, the one who so desperately expected from me what I expected from him.

In my helplessness, I went – I ran – to Kondász for some tripe. Old man Kondász is dead, but his table remains unoccupied, and they put a pint of beer there for him, his 'pitcher and a dash'. Ever since Marika and that other have taken the place over, they make tripe like in Hódmezővásárhely, let's say, soupy, and nothing on the side, just a slice of bread. The bartender was called Marika, almost seven feet tall, with a ready laugh and blond hair, a frogman, they say, and he was happy when they called him Marika, he loved fine things, when he saw my pretty blue and green scarf, he looked at me as if we were both under water, he caressed, he caressed the scarf, pinching it between his fingers, sizing it up, so to speak, oh, my dear, this is *truly* divine, cashmere, Marika, I said cruelly, he waited till I put down my mug, then called after me, charming as can be, fifty per cent cashmere, honey, but very nice all the same.

Now he was weighing the tripe.

I didn't recognize Portugál at first, despite his forty-two years he looked like an old man when he was renovating the house already, he was a little gone in the head, it was said, in the events following '56 he saw proof that God himself had become a commie, and this weakened him body and soul, he worked hard but got little done, he went from sloshed to sozzled in half an afternoon, he slept out at the building site, covering himself with cement bags, when I realized I said nothing to anyone, just left the blanket outside the house for him.

He's grown thinner since, with a sour smell, they started hushing, be quiet, Portugál spat on the floor, licked the corner of his lips, his pink gums, looked at me, and broke into a song, first more like talking, his voice trembling, trying himself out, gradually his body changing, too, he straightened up and grew taller, a tall man! I never noticed how tall, that he had any *tallness* to him, his voice, too, stronger and stronger, clear even if throaty, bending, floating, the tavern listening in a trance, I see that the song of this ragged old man is about how he can't be trampled underfoot, that even he is incapable of trampling himself underfoot, you, Bohush, know a lot of men like that, I know, instead of that heap of rags I saw a man and an artist, what this Portugál had been before and after his song.

We clapped, and on a sudden whim I stroked him, my hand slipping from the top of his head down his greasy hair to the sandpaper-like neck, I leaned my head against his, and we stayed like that for a moment, then Portugál backed off, let me go! he hissed, I smiled, though I saw how angry he was, you smell! you're a smelly woman! leave me alone! he ran out to the backyard, don't be angry with him, honey, said Marika, he's going to die, lung cancer, he's hawking up phlegm, at which point, I don't know why, but I started laughing, I was shaken by an irresistible, crude, strange, stubborn laughter, I hawked, guffawed, shook my hair, as the men, spent and well into their cups, looked on in expectation.

In which case, I'd better do a quick disappearing act, I thought.

Our children sensed that something was up, and put each other to bed. We were sitting in the kitchen again. And then my husband suddenly raised his head from his plate of tripe, shook himself as if he had just woken up, and took my hand. Like the Lapp shaman woman, that's what he was like. Bohumil! He's my man, Bohumil! Looking at me earnestly, like that young handyman in the afternoon, every part of him laughing, I see, something's gotten through to him, I see, his eyes laughing silently, his brow, his hair . . .

He grinned. Well?! he said. Well, what? Does that mean? And he shrugged. Well . . . I said. See? he said, still holding my hand. I nodded, with relatively few tears in my eyes.

I was happy. We sat like that for a long time. When he decided to speak it was no good, in his joy he over-reacted, he acted superior at my expense. But I could also feel that something had happened at last; the only thing we could realistically expect, that's what happened, a miracle. Still, he shouldn't chat away like that, it's going to be me lying there again. And I told him so. He looked at me gravely, deadly serious, he may even have turned pale, he was visibly struggling with his words, if . . . if you want . . . if that's how you want it . . . then . . . then I will have this baby now.

I slapped him lightly. In our joy, we ignored everyone and everything. Meanwhile, he kept stroking my hand, my arms. He was sly, though, touching me so that my body would be guaranteed to respond. Calculating, but who cares. And he was right, for the first time in days (weeks) my body felt alive.

Dear Bohumil. Silence. I am lying in the dark, dreaming over you, 'my melancholy baby'. You are one of my outstanding assets. *Hold it, hold it. Once more. Try again.* If I were twenty years younger or twenty years older, I'd leave everything behind, and move to Prague, *temporarily*, into some *ulice* or other, maybe I'd rent a small apartment on some *naměsti* overlooking some *mosts*, and you would come over every afternoon – and stop that whining, it won't help you – between three and six, read to me what you had written that day, then leave. But hold on, damn it, why should I be the one to wait? Why shouldn't you wait from time to time, pacing up

126

and down, stuffing your kittens to the bursting point. By the way, I really don't mean to hike my price up, but there are days when my eyes are like a kitten's. You mustn't expect me to be honest with you, though. On the other hand, I'd buy a barrel of old Brno beer, and we'd make *short shrift* of it. Which reminds me: I am exactly of the age I should be at, and I think I can safely say that I always have been.

Want me to walk all over you? I know that's what you like. I'd swamp you with, yes, I'd make a present to you of my jealousy. At first this would please you, then it would not please you. You'd see that I see when you can't wait to go. You'd see that I see when you would cry. (I know, I know: the male principle! A man's tears!) You'd see that I see when you feel like being alone . . . And once you see that I see, it's all the same what I do, right away, everything is *offensive*.

I'd accuse you because of your sentences. I'd point my dagger at your heart and accuse you of wanting nothing else except sentences. Not even me, just the sentences coming out of me. But be advised, a *madame* like me, from Pest, has a way of settling in a soul! I see myself, a botch work of sentences, just an alloy, I know. But with a bit of *hochmetz* I might say: Orpheus and Eurydice! You writers work with borrowed material. That's what your lives are like. In which case, my life is like this. A printed upper-case letter in a novel. A straight line, a curve, the dot over the *i*. But I don't want you inventing me, too. Not *me*! I'd rather not have you love me at all. Though I'm not saying yet you should go to hell.

Sooner or later I'd confess that I'm not really jealous of you. Of you I'm not jealous, only of my husband. It's not like I thought it would be twenty years ago, but neither is it the way they say . . . He gets all the sentences from me he possibly can . . . and he always will, I think . . . And you probably know what a Hungarian sentence is like, Bohumil, with not a structure in sight, or a decent relative pronoun, the words lumped all together, and yet . . . A Hungarian sentence is this 'and yet'. You have to start from scratch every time. It's as little civilized as the heart. On my birthday he asked me to dance, and I saw by his dance steps . . . by the steps . . . that he never stepped this way before, and then the evening was over, and I waited for him to fall asleep, and then lay on top of him with my full length, I wanted to be very heavy, like a stone, and I was very heavy, like a stone, and I pressed down on this man under me, and cried him to tatters, with nothing but my damned-silly-woman's tears, and I wanted to be inside him with the power of a stone. (Whether he woke up or not I don't know, and what's more, I don't even care.)

It's adventurous, Bohush, living with a man like this through a whole lifetime. There was a moment, about ten years ago, when I thought I knew what the future would bring. It was maddening, though I thought of nothing but good things. Now it's different, now I've got to be inquisitive about things, including my husband. But in the long run, it's rough going, him being him and me being me. It's very hard to accept. If he were me, I'd manage it between me and myself. But the short-distance stuff doesn't interest me. It's not going to be easy, getting rid of me, Bohumil. Or it'll go so smoothly, you won't even notice. Think about that. A slip of the tongue, it's too late, you, dear heart, just don't go getting any thoughts into your head, you hear? Do you believe in God? Were you a good husband? A feather-fingered pianist in a side street of Liben. We'd just sit there, and I'd find myself wanting you.

Do you see at last, you obstinate wild man, how I love you? *Like this*. Not faithfully, not vigorously, not very much, just like *this*. Let's not rush anything.

I am a wife, emphasis on all four words. I've just thought of a kind of crustacean again, stewed in curry and nutmeg; I'm going to feed you, I told you before.

At dawn this morning the sea, the home of the crustacean, was a very special silvery-pink in tone, then powder-blue, and until just now greyish-brown, all of Budapest was reflected in it, the entire turn-of-the-century concept. In other words, Prague, with all those towers. We'd find the 'direction of our hearts' (you said it), and put an end to the bleakness of our cities.

Or should we also climb way up the chimney? You'd pull yourself up, and as if unawares, put one hand on your hip, the other to your eye, well I'll be darned, little lady, you'd say appreciatively, what a *beobachtungstelle*, or observation post, this would make. You mean a look-out tower, I'd add. Heck, no! A look-out tower, that's for civilians, miss, an observation post, or *beobachtungstelle*, that's for the military, the military in action that must keep an eye on the movement of enemy troops. You're such a clever, fine-looking young woman, miss, but if Captain Tonser were to hear you say that, he'd twirl his sabre at you and yell, 'I'm gonna fuck your cooch to shreds!' Bohoushek, I'd expand on it, though, hanging both feet into the airshaft. For crying out loud, now why would you wanna fuck my cooch to shreds? It's me you loved, I used to carry your sword for you! you'd holler with a full throat, leaning over me, and your expression would be threatening, like the gargoyles at the top of cathedrals. And where has it got you? I'd ask with a superior shrug. Isn't it fantastic, Bohumil? I'd feast my eyes on the gently sloping countryside surrounded by hills and woods, I'd survey our cities . . .

Should I buy mauve tights? Crimson? Smokey-grey? Red-wood? – There is no darkness in me. I love the light, and the light loves me, while you, dear heart, would understand, standing, standing there in the sun, you'd understand me standing in the door opening unto the garden, squinting, all those wrinkles running up and down your face, like an old woman's, I've seen photographs, so don't try to deny it, besides, I meant it as a compliment, this old woman, in your younger days, I see, you weren't averse to a little seduction, thanks a lot! oh, the roguish Hrabal of the thousand faces and masks and the mask as a human face, oh! Hrabal the gardener, Hrabal the man of passion, Hrabal the indifferent, Hrabal the man of the street, Hrabal the beer drinker, on one of the photos holding a woman's hand, not mine, my age, though, more or less, greying at the temples, refined, but don't tell her I said so, looking at you with adoration, in love, obviously, I love it when they love you, plus the ten nails, if you remember, you're so strong, calm and substantial on these pictures, I could trust myself to you, you'd stand squinting in the doorway, giving the garden the once-over, in fact, and then – and then, under an unlikely-red, flaming-red – this is where the red-wood colour would come in, bush, who would you see, dear Bohumil? you'd see me, my dear, a *distant, sizzling hot* female body basking in the sun, the sunlight would come pouring down on me so I'd grow dizzy, like a sledge-hammer, I wouldn't know where I was, circles vibrating behind my eyelids, it's nice here in No Man's Land, you'd break into a grin, and stand there like that, awkwardly, on No Man's Land, like me. You think if I put a sentence into the conjunctive mode it's no longer true? When this light leaves me, I swear, dying out even for a moment, the sun can shine up there, I'm lost in the dark . . . feeling my way with outstretched arms, as if wandering in the moonless night. Or

130

as if I were a bird without wings. My husband used to stand there, too, holding in his hand, as if it were a lance, his pen, to protect himself with. My pet likes to think of himself this way. (It is my usual mistake at such times to ask him out to sunbathe. He could cry at such idiocy, he says.)

What would happen, what would have happened, if my husband had decided to write about Fontane instead? He's showing off all the time anyway with how he loves me like *Theodar*, it makes me laugh, it's the one thing he can't do, he could only lie like Theodor, and he's hanging his nose all day about Effi Briest dying, that he's read the novel again, and she went and died again. (And how he should be writing an essay entitled 'The Linear Book of Lies', in which he'd show up this kind of accommodating American novel for what it was, the East Coast! technique + exhibitionism + easy consumption, sincerity as a means.) So you see, I am not alone. Still, I need you. I couldn't say what you mean to me, but I miss you. The meaning of 'I – miss – you' is not (or not only) 'you are missing from inside me', but: 'I am your miss of the sea-blue-eyes' (I am the Miss, or gal, for you). Also, I am going to paint a tree blue for you, an entire tree blue for you, you will get to chose the spot, either here on the plane, or at Mondsee or the Moldva, above the Manes, by the dam, where again and again the swans attempts to swim upstream, against the current . . . It's going to be a painstaking labour of love, the entire trunk with a brush filched from the kids . . .

The house is chock full of you. A Czech ghost, no big deal . . . Even where the bricks should be, it's you. A stranger in the house. They tell me that in your opinion, people don't sing any more. So let me. *A lovely day in May is dawning / Not a drop of dew on the awning* – or the other way around: *Dew sits heavy on the awning / A lovely May-day is dawning* . . . You've got a musical streak, played the E-flat trumpet, I'm told.

I'm lying down. The ocean is black now, sparkling ebony-black. Where are you? You're nowhere, just all talk, or not even that. What do you want from me? Do you want anything from me? Stay where you are, then, shut up in your room in Prague, slamming the keys of your Perkeo typewriter, clicketty-clack, God forbid you should get out! oh, it's vital, what you're doing, that art of yours, that great big bamboozling Central European *joie de vivre*! Well, I'll have you know: I don't give a damn about your Central Europe, it doesn't even exist! it's all in your head, so let it stay there, and you inside your prefab flat, sitting on your ass, in which case, though, you should at least have the common decency not to pass in and out of my window like this. Where are you, anyhow? Why are you *postponing* me? There's nothing but darkness now, the black ocean of Budapest.

I can't keep up this letter writing forever, you know. Fine, have it your way. Love me casually, or because you're curious, because you're not paying attention, because it makes the time pass. That's it: simply, *plainly*, just to make the time pass. Love on the Great Hungarian Plain. This would be your Hungarian connection.

Silence. I am lying in the dark. My body is growing tired, with sudden flashes of pain starting up, merry little streams, everybody taking advantage of my strength, my husband the only exception, he takes advantage of my weakness, too. And how are you planning to do it, Bohumil, I wonder?

I see, I can see that I am needed here. Except that sometimes

I think it's *some*body that's needed, and not me, an anonymous jack-of-all-trades, lover, wife, a family, a secretary, a mother, a mother-surrogate, interior decorator, cook, salad boy, spiritual councellor, proof-reader and gardener, telephone girl, nanny, cleaning lady, friend, all rolled into one, buy one, get one hundred, the Portrait of a Housewife, a Neapolitan farce, the milk boiling over and the kid getting a clout on the back of the head at one and the same time, at the same time, the mailman not getting a tip by oversight, the smallest one swimming in the chicken soup (don't be lazy, flip those legs!), talking with my melancholy daddy on the phone, and in the *meantime*, in a foreign language, with someone else, from Munich, while creating a linear grid for figuring our percentages, this arm-in-arm with my son, without the faintest idea of what we are doing, thereby eliciting his scorn and disdain, and finally, amidst tears and laughter, collapsing into 'the legion of unwashed dishes' and blubbering in summation: I want to get published, too (applause).

I am the Great Subsitute, a great honour, no doubt, everything that is not, that is what I am. But I am.

The decision was mine to make. I am free and I am tethered, that is my state of being.

There is inside me, in the pit of my stomach, or my shoulder, or in my lap really, something small, the size of my fist, something that is . . . alive. The thing live in me is faith. Dense, bright, sometimes dark, and then it is thick, heavy. There is belief in me, belief in this man, belief in my children, my girls, my boys, belief in this fourth, in My Little Dilemma, that's going to be my pet name for it, My Little Dilemma, I believe in our garden, the hysterically lush pear tree, the nearby poplars, the head cheese, the nappies, the fillings in the teeth, the blues, the beer, the bed, our friends, the pebbles, my dearly departed ones, the stars . . . I gaze at the sky, all velvety mist and silver hues, I think with sympathy about the *old* light of the stars, yet now I know I am not alone, not even in the midst of so many people, though possibly these stars have already died out, only their brightness still travelling, towards me, existing only in the light of my eyes, so I may see them, only in this light can I believe, this light that is not, the light of something that is not, this light from the infinite, this light is in my eyes – in short, I believe that in the final analysis there is nothing but this distant belief, as it is written, 'in the infinite, and within the infinite, even in the fate of the tiniest speck of dust', amen.

He is sleeping next to me, happy; I love to be in bed with him, my husband. He looks contented, tired, exhausted from work, like an animal. I look at his face, spent, wasted, I look at the deep furrows on his brow, his beehive head of hair, he is calm, he is sleeping calmly. And I am restless. I don't know what I am thinking.

And then, in this state of helplessness, there boomed from very close up a ship's fog horn, the garden reaches down to the sea, if there were no fog, or the hedges pruned back further, I could see it pass by the house, bright, festooned with Chinese lanterns, like a giant mammoth, like in that Fellini film, and prompted by the cosmic sound of the retreating boat's fog horn I suddenly realized that no, I do not love him now, I do not love him in the least, so much so that it has gone beyond not loving, it is more than that. They are sleeping, breathing peacefully by my side, and around me, in my bed, in the other room – those that are mine. This man is the man of my life, and I don't want to look at him. What is this meanness? That everything is concrete, is that it? I feel something that even love can't remedy. There is no touching it, no getting around it. I have tripped up. I am not a coward, but I am scared, though I have been intimidated, yet I would like to cry, but there's no reason why, yet something's gone wrong, very wrong, just the same. What should I change when everything is in order? Everything is in order, except the whole thing is not in order, and if the whole thing is not in order, I am not in order. I close my eyes: it is bad . . . My eyelashes flutter: it is bad. I scratch my forehead: it is bad. When I do something bad: it is bad. I stare into the emptiness with benumbed, wide-open eyes. What's to come? The terrible moment of the insatiable lack of desire.

I do not think about death, except when thinking of my mother-in-law. Since she passed away there's been no one to help me, to support me, no one to tell me, not once, honey, I wouldn't wear that today, if I were you, don't you know it's spring! No, there is no one to take care of me, it's me, taking care of them all. Maybe you're out there, Bohumil, but without me. I have nothing to do with the whole thing. My arm hurts, feels like it's gonna break off. 'Forgive me, Lord, that I have withered,' this was written on my mother-in-law's death notification, I want the same on mine.

I am in the dark. I am sitting in the sun. It throbs, it throbs. I am one.

What has been left out is also everything.

Mám rada. I love you.

   With hugs and kisses, Sulamith of the Ashen Hair, Yes.

Chapter Three

'Heaven is not humane,
nor is the man who thinks.'
Hrabal

What's there left to tell? He had a rotten night and he woke up feeling rotten. He was dead tired and his eye hurt. He suspected it was conjunctivitis and stood in front of the mirror eyeing himself for some time, eyeing his eyes, the eyeballs covered with a thin layer of mucus, which here and there bunched up into small yellowish, or rather, colourless and translucent globs. Blinking, he tried to force the mucus to bunch up in one spot. He rolled his eyes, badly bloodshot. It's at times like this that the experienced man says: a blood-red horizon, wind's in the offing.

The silence was penetrating.

He did not want his mother to see he was morose, it wasn't worth it; he was lucky if he got off with a simple chiding (as if his bad mood was the same as *being* bad, or as if it was a sign of malice or a lack of talent – though there is something to be said for that); but it was even worse when she tried to remedy the situation. His mother was getting on his nerves more and more, lately. Sometimes he felt he couldn't even recognize her, that only her clothes served as a point of reference. Her walk had turned ungainly along with her figure, and her hair and skin had changed, too, which he put down to old age. But he had not expected that his mother would change inside as well, would start using different words – that her soul would change, that not only her eyes would change, but her glance as well. That this should also be put down to old age surprised him.

His mother had always been strong, carrying the family on her shoulder; now she was strong and weak, appearing tough and selfish. But at the same time, she'd start whimpering for no apparent reason. This irritated him no end, even though he was quite capable of crying along with humans at the drop of a hat.

'Good morning, mother,' he said as he entered the kitchen, and quickly embraced her so she shouldn't see his face (shouldn't see his true colours). His mother had never been tall, but now she was shorter, still, and somehow harder to the touch (from shrinking in height?). But it still felt good embracing her, and when he thought that some day he would no longer stand in the kitchen like this with this woman in his arms – actually, he couldn't even think it, and that's the truth. His mother's odour had changed, too, an unpleasant, bitter smell coming from her scalp, so he released her.

'How did you sleep, son?' This did not call for an answer. The breakfast took its start, the battle in which the woman insisted on every insignificant nook and cranny, a hand-to-hand combat for every available inch of space, wanting to make everything her own, every feeling, every word uttered, the sugar cubes, the future, firing questions at him. She also wanted to own their hopes. They made a well-rehearsed duo. While the son put up the coffee, the mother did the same for the tea; they were never in each other's way, they always knew whose turn it was to move, constantly watching each other, askance, with a reprimand always on hand – did you sprinkle the bread? because, in accordance with an old custom, they warmed the bread up in the oven *just a little*; one set the table while the other fumbled with the napkins.

He did not want this hand-to-hand combat with his mother any more, but was forced into it time and again, though their squabbles had no purpose, which made them irritating and, above all, something to be avoided. But there was no avoiding them. The combat was gone, but the nagging remained. He liked this morning's embrace about his mother, this one movement, this was left, this was the love of a child, this single movement, and this movement, too, was his. In old age we become not wise and mature, but barren, bald, bare, it's not the late golden light that glimmers, but the embers that stink. He saw the colours fade out of his mother, and what was left, too – the petty-mindedness and the cosmic depression. Partly his fault, obviously. He thought of the poet Vörösmarty, wine and Beckett, and distilled spirits. What's at stake here?

And he needed to talk to Hrabal.

He had to think of Anna. And then again. He spread butter on his toast. He laid his manuscript out, fan-like, on the table, turning the pages filled with writing – his 'report'. He loved Anna.

'Don't munch your food,' his mother said severely, at which he said what he always said, that he wasn't munching, it was the green pepper *crunching* between his teeth. His mother waved this off and started on the dishes, which her son hated more than anything, this busy-bodying, the way she practically swiped the plate from under his nose, the last hindrance to washing-up.

He loved Anna's tabby-cat eyes, her motley-coloured

glance. He loved Anna's high spirits, her strength, her confidence. He loved everything about her. Her songs, too, he loved, writing most of them off to her credit as prayers. He had a soft spot for the blues to begin with. The choir of angels could hardly suppress their sneers, even though it was not the social woes that he loved in this music, not the complaining that dovetailed with the acceptance of life, but the improvisational warmth, the 'dirty tones', Bessie Smith's 'pained instability'. Yet it soon turned out that in this respect, if in no other, compared to him the angels were petty monarchs, courtiers, gentlefolk. Privileged. He was more plebeian than any of them.

From the infinitive subjectivity of the dark, blue-black sky he glanced at Anna one last time. The infanticide, you should excuse the expression, she just barely avoided (with a little help). And now there she lay in the night, her eyes vacuous. 'Everything had moved from its appointed place and had overlapped, everything that is *not*. It was a matter of *material* suffering, what else. NO NEED FOR NAMES.' The *keserves*, or lamenting song, means for the Hungarians what the blues does for Americans. He was proud of this discovery, and for this and for no other reason did he prefer the *Kurucz* to the *Labancz*. The anti-Habsburg *Kurucz* soldiers knew how to cry into their wine, not like those pro-Habsburg *Labancz*. (The Hungarian blues notes, by the way, are called the 'Transdanubian third'. The third of the closing note is either minor, or major, or in-between . . .)

He thought this woman (this Hungarian woman) beautiful, even tantalizing. If I were to court her, he thought frivolously, I'd do it with the *Song of Songs*. I'd cheat and say I wrote it.

'A woman's got to be finished,' he mumbled to himself, just like a presumptuous old suitor, then cautiously tried that 'throaty *Sprechgesang*' (cf. Pierrot Lunaire, 1912, Europe), *parlante* talking blues whose greatest master, perhaps, was little Carlsson from the cold-cold north, who, until overtaken by 'the great European silence', talked and talked, scattering words about; he talked and he did not, but even his silence was a kind of talk, spreading about him words and the silences between words that were of equal rank, this was his magic, this Swedish nonsense, the throbbing of emptiness, or as he said, this *lanovka* to silence. The avalanche of silence. And in rough translation the famous line: Nestle the surface of your face in the pit of my shoulder, do! (see P. Anka's adaptation.)

He was embarrassed to notice – because she seemed to have one up on him here – that Anna had started praying.

A part of humanity, possibly the more ingenious part, wasn't quite clear about whether 'Christian culture stood under the sign of happiness, as Jewish culture surely did not, yet there was agreement that the mutual relationship of the conceptual triumvirate of *love, suffering* and *happiness*, which were of equal rank, stood in the centre. And that in this relationship the mutuality is indissoluble, which means that they cannot be replaced by any other concepts.' These reflections are from Sadan, of whom Thomas Mann writes with such respect; he thinks that this wise man, this fascinating thinker is of Norwegian stock, but as far as I know he's from Burma, though an incorrigible European. Sadan can posit neither a correlation nor a differentiation between happiness and joy, or joy and suffering. Thus, happiness is not the fulfilment of joy (the experiment in everyday language to substitute one for the other – is this not one of the things that helped make twentieth-century culture so unstable?); nor is happiness the total absence of suffering, but the fulfilment of love. The Lord was in agreement here.

Listening to the sorrowful prayer, he laughed a bittersweet laugh. He'd walked into the boobie-trap of his own making again. He liked to forget about this boobie-trap, the fact that he was incapable of reducing the suffering of humans, because only humans can reduce the suffering of humans. This animated everything on Earth, this painful paradox.

He was not otherwise displeased with his creation, but for contradictions he had no love, or rather, he loved, poor thing, everything and everyone, that's how he had invented himself, this was the *clue*, and in the long-run, his hobby-horse. But he was not crazy about these theoretical, moral and cosmetological Moebius strips, the unlooked-for refractions of the good and the bad, the fact that the perfection of the world should consist of this balance instead of its perfection. (At the same time, though, it was with no small delight in mischief that he read the lucubrations of Milena Cound Erasmus, the professor of literature from Karlovi Vary, according to whom the idea that the devil was the champion of Evil and the angels the champions of the Good is angelic demagogy, because mastery of the world is shared by the devils and the angels equally; furthermore, most of the world is rooting not for an angelic victory, but for the shared balance of these two powers.) The world, and this should come as no surprise, he considered to be the shadow of himself; as a consequence, all this filled him with a bit of uneasiness. But to speak plainly: it pained him to be forced to admit that the *gist of creation*, its bone and marrow, is not the Bach-Tolstoy-Euclidean line, but the Mozart-Dostoyevksy-Gödel lobby. (He kept Goethe separate; essentially, he did not consider him as part of creation . . .) In short, though he created man in his image, the dimension of the world (its diamond axis) was angelic.

And so he loved the world he had created, especially Albert Einstein, whose ambition, even, he loved, though in this matter he had felt compelled to give him a rap on the knuckles (cf.: theory of relativity). Albert had a little four-line ditty that made him a special favourite, an insubstantial thing, no more than the intake of breath, about the fact that independently of the theory of relativity, the stars followed their paths for ever and ever in accordance with Newton's axioms.

His mother's latest pretensions were coupled with a surprising intellectual liveliness which though her son might have regarded as inauthentic, still, he could not ignore altogether. This was not a sign of old age, or if it was, it was a surprising sign, unaccountable.

It took the Lord considerably more time to develop a liking for Heisenberg; he was hurt that this guy had such a good nose for sniffing out the uncertainty principle. At the bottom of his heart, he preferred the Greeks. The force of gravity is the Lord's creation, and therefore needs no further study. That's clear thinking. And geometry is the combination of logic and beauty. Ditto. But that it's not the particle moving wave-like, but the probability of its presence?! Come now! The effect which, thumbing its nose, struts about in front of the cause . . . OK, wise guys, gimme one good reason why you can't measure mass and speed at the same time?!

'Just because! Just because!' his mother screeched, drunk on her triumph. 'That's how it is! And if that's how it is, it's better you should know, know that you can't know, know that there's no safe harbour to drop your anchor . . .'

She gave her son a look of malicious glee. He went berserk. He refused to make *this sort of distinction* between knowing and not knowing, it was vainglorious, and vainglory is the domain of the devil. The 'divine meandering' holds true only when considered along with its detours, while Satan is the *or*. Separation. Wheeling-dealing. Flight. Dualism. Satan is form and content. Anything *but* the proof of God. Those he places in opposition in this manner are to hide behind. That's what Satan's got to offer, this hideout; he's turning the world into a tunnel and a labyrinth; hide, he whispers, there are things that are not of God, see, I am one myself, lack-of-God, a hole. Satan is the great crossword puzzle solver, offering the puzzle as opposed to the secret, the story as opposed to the event, nostalgia as opposed to remembrance.

'Whereas there is no hiding!'

'Don't be a fool, son. That upright Heisenberg is talking about matter, not two, but one. Life itself consists of waking and sleeping and the dream of truth is falsehood. Besides, I enjoy solving a crossword puzzle myself now and then.'

'Satan is he who deconstructs, who disunites. He's the one who talks about cleanliness and filth, light and shade. No. There is no up and there is no down, there is no man and there is no woman, there is no big and there is no little . . .'

'All right, all right . . . Overplaying your hand as usual. Is there nothing *solid* in you. I'm fed up. To have to . . . even in my old age, to . . . for the thousandth time . . . You're always in such a rush. You can't wait. Waiting. Isn't that the noblest faculty?'

'Mother, please. Would you kindly refrain from adorning yourself with other people's feathers.'

'It's no big deal, seeing how . . . But come to think of it, I don't understand . . .'

'I know!'

'I don't understand. There's Satan, and then there's you. And already, that makes two, and not one. Or am I mistaken?'

'No. Everything converges in me. Everything that is, and everything that is not, is in me. I am like a novel. In this novel all those who are at a great distance from each other but belong together meet. All is one. Not identical, not the same. What differs, differs. But it's inside me. As one.'

143

'Indeed?' his mother said, arching her eyebrows.

'I am that I am.'

'Look, son, keep that for the reporters . . . Though now that we're on the subject, let me ask, as your mother. Granted, you are that you are. But who *are* you? Who is that you? Who?!'

He fell silent. His mother had triumphed.

'You're a conservative!' she shrieked. 'Newton is out! You got along splendidly, but it's over and done with!' she preached with neophyte zeal. They were tired. The Lord tried to listen to Anna's prayer. His mother took out a crossword puzzle. The Lord had made her a dictionary, with an eye for completeness and that's not nothing, as they'd say in Hungarian, but even more so in offhand Budapest slang. So here it is:

. . . calculo	= minimo
. . . fallaci	= oriana
all . . .	= though
Asian language	= urdu
bird like a seagull	= tern
Brazilian writer	= amado
bridge in Venice	= rialto
Bulgarian name (man's)	= hristo
cormorant	= fisher
creeper	= haricot
Croatian inventor	= tesla
Dalmatian island	= vis
einsteinium	= ein
elephant bone	= ivory
embarrassment	= chagrin
English beer	= ale
europium	= eu

fashionable	= uptodate
former de Gaulle party	= UNR
former king of the Goths	= alarik
French actor-director	= tati
further . . .	= more
GDR in French	= RDA
girlfriend of János Vajda (poet)	= gina
green mineral	= jade
Israeli airline	= elal
Italian painter	= tiepolo
modugno pop-song	= volare
moral evil	= vice
mutton with rice	= pilaf
mythological figure	= satyr
old rank	= palatine
Papal curse	= anathema
poet Ady's pseudonym	= yda
Polish mini-bus	= nysa
principle	= idea
privative (suffix, foreign)	= un
river in Vilna	= ?
schnapps (of juniper)	= gin
Slav gentleman	= pan
Slav name (man's)	= petar
sly	= sneaky
Sumerian city	= ur
Svejk's army pastor	= katz
toi et . . .	= *moi*
trade . . .	= union
Traven's novel	= deathship
woman's garment	= bra
woodland deity	= pan
young animal	= kid

When the lanky Gödel popped up with his strange theories, he gradually accepted the fact that people had come to realize something. This news, too, came from his mother, who got a real kick out of intellectual scandal. Next to Gödel, Giordano Bruno was her favourite.

'What a blast! What characters! Gödel a *maitre d'* in Békés County, but he was banished from there, so he ordered two cabs, that's how he went to Lake Balaton, he in one cab, his hat in the other . . . But what was I saying? Oh, yes. That if the system is free of contradictions, then, son, it contains a predication or two you're helpless against, you can't prove it, you can't disprove it. On the other hand, if within a system every predication is susceptible to proof, then the system is of necessity contradictory. There's always some howler, son. And don't tell me that this is not a pleasant thought . . .

'Sure,' he nodded without much conviction. From time to time he got bored with humans, and then he preferred to think of some other creatures, the dandelion, or the Man from Mars. Or Bolyai's geometry. He felt bad about that awkward affair with Gauss. Though bored may not be the appropriate word: maybe he just needed a rest.

While Anna was praying, the writer was not praying, but the Lord accepted this as prayer, too, and rightly so, may I add. The writer was afraid to pray. He was ashamed because he'd always end up pestering the Lord for something, but what was even more embarrassing – and this he wouldn't have liked to admit to anyone, be he an earthly or heavenly vicar, in short, that once again the gist of said pestering would have been the fact that the writer would have much preferred to be a good writer than a good Catholic; this is what he would have preferred to take out long-term loans on, and to top it off (in accordance with not-admitting again), he'd have done so with pride because, with pretended humility, he believed that he'd end up serving the Lord *anyway* with his work. Who had a good laugh at this; there's enough and then some of *his* type, people who are neither true believers nor true non-believers. He was slightly annoyed, though, that the writer shied away from faith itself. He wanted it and wanted it not (thinking, foolish man, that it was up to him), seeing some *trick* in faith, a ruse, but at the very least appeasement, some petty or large-scale deal (Pascal! Pascal!). He shied away from being broken in, like a domestic animal, afraid that he'd never even notice the insidious undermining of his independence. Yet he went largely uncontaminated by this century's emancipatory ferment; he understood and hoped to achieve a dependence that was free; to belong to someone while retaining his freedom.

He wanted to be faithful and knew how to go about it, but he did not want to be a faithful dog, he dreaded that. Yet he often considered Catholics, among whom he numbered himself, as precisely such faithful dogs, whose sole arrogant and generally successful striving was to suppress the Pharisaic urge that had embedded itself in everything (everything that was *them*).

'You're a fool, son.' The Lord waved him off. 'Though I know what you mean.'

I heard somewhere in company that every man is a separate word; consequently, mankind put together is the language, or book, that the Lord reads; one word cannot understand another, for meaning is contained in language, and he who understands this is not the writer, but the reader; he studies, he savours the words, fiddles with them, stylizes them, slaps them around, an active reader deletes, reorganizes, rewrites, turns back the pages, skips ahead. The question raises itself: what kind of a reader is the Lord? A lousy one, if the boredom and impatience are real. On the other hand, shouldn't we applaud every kind of reader in this post-modern world of ours, especially if he's the only one? And what kind of a writer would the Lord make, now that we're on the subject? None at all. The Lord penning it? Oh, come now! He who remembers it all does not write; he is either a monster, or he is the Lord God; possibly the Lord God is a monster, this latter possibility, though, I'd rather not pursue because of the forgiveness spiel (I say this as a private man). God alone is capable of forgiveness while forgetting nothing, while he who remembers nothing is either a rascal or a half-wit. The writer is in between the two, between the all and the nothing, the monster and the rascal, the Lord and the half-wit, one time this, another time that, neither this nor that, nothing, a great big nothing. That infamous student of Lotman, the patron and unsolicited shyster of the Prague school of linguistics, Inskij, says that writers were created after the Fall, when man's intellect dulled and he knew evil, and felt a propensity for it. John Phil is of the opinion that all of man's capabilities have fallen into sin, everything that should have served the overall fulfilment of the created world. This fall put an end to the authenticity and reality of the world, this fall made possible the existence of writers, so they could roll up their sleeves and attempt their mighty and wonderful and completely hopeless task.

Anna (a word in the process of being read) reached the end of her prayer.

'Of course, my child, go on, love him,' the Lord responded to the indirect question of the prayer without really thinking, but due to the above-mentioned structure of the world, he was not able to let Anna know directly. Seeing his mother's disapproving glance (for one thing, what sort of omnipotence is this, for another, what will your Father have to say to such rashness), he exploded, why must you stick your nose into everything, mother, and in the same breath also apologized, forgive me, mother; too late, his mother slammed down the crossword puzzle, and deeply offended, stormed out of the kitchen, while he washed the morning dishes again; when it came to the dishes he trusted no one, least of all his mother.

He was not obsessed with taking up arms, but for Anna he wished to do something, a woman's got to be finished, he repeated to himself. Out of sorts, he sloshed around in the dishwater. When he was out of sorts he liked to watch the building of the church tower at Ulm, overseeing the work again and again, though only superficially, the quality of the materials, the expertise, the stone tracery – the stone tracery invisible to everyone except to him and the stonemasons.

The stonemasons knew this, too.

The legend that man is closest to God at the top of the church tower of Ulm must have originated from this. (At any rate, I did my bit and climbed up; of the 768 steps mentioned by the guide books I counted 761, then, with trembling knees sat for a long time by the bank of the Danube, trying to imagine a water molecule, a particle of water, reaching Budapest, and even beyond . . .) There were stories, too, of over-ambitious Jacob Stieger, Staircase Jacob, the young apprentice, who insisted on being present at the completion of the church – close to God! – and then plunged to his death with the whole town watching. He fell like so much dead weight. Even if we ignore air resistance, it's still over five seconds! A town that for five long seconds thinks about life and death – no wonder the Lord had a soft spot for Ulm.

But he did not love, no, he could not love the face of young Jacob the moment his hand lost its desperate grip on the stone tracery and he began to fall. This face was not the face of terror, nor the face of ambition; this face was the face of disappointment, of emptiness, and thus of hatred. This face did not belong to him. Bury the surface of your face in the pit of my shoulder, do. No–no–no–no! No! Not for five seconds. It's not worth it. *Amor sui usque ad contemptum Dei* (Love of self verging on contempt for the Lord), says St Augustine, who thought of everything. But did he ever think, thought the Lord, what would happen if we put a Dei in place of the sui? Words.

Infinity, of which more hereafter, had the disadvantage, the drawback, among others, that the days had a way of blending into one another, a Tuesday, by way of example, could be a Wednesday at the drop of a hat – with this in mind, all this happened on the day when a courageous man from Copenhagen, by the name of Mandyguard, asked the Lord in his own gruff, low-key, café style, or rather, decided that he really *ought* to ask the Lord, his humour, whatever happened to his sense of humour? This I would love to ask him myself, otherwise, I'd let him be. Let him sit to his heart's content by the table of a café or a restaurant, out on a terrace, in a cinema's foyer, on the bleachers of a soccer field, in a church on the outskirts of town.

If he won't feel like talking, though, I'll understand.

After a while, we'd take our leave. He'd go his way, I'd go mine.

*

> 'Man employs a multiplicity of means towards a single end; God makes use of a single means for a multiplicity of ends.'
> Gustav Theodor Fechner

Man uses a variety of metaphors to refer to the world, and

'this is reckless and irresponsible'. As the African proverb says, words are just dandy, but it takes a hen to lay an egg. The Good Lord was omnipotent; there was one thing, though, he could not do, he could not play the saxophone. Offhand it would be hard to say why. Once upon a time he ignored the industrious, inventive Belgian Adolphe Sachs; he thought the clarinet filled the bill, and did not for a moment believe that there might be a missing link in the assembly of musical instruments.

Like all beings, he too had a driving ambition to surpass himself, but since he was the most with the mostest, it took no small measure of ingenuity and recklessness on his part to allay said ambition. In any event, he was attracted by what he did not know. Ultimately, herein lies the motive force of all creation (the prime mover). Truth is always concrete, said some German or other at a later date. The Good Lord was drawn to the story. The story. He wanted a story.

He was surrounded by an infinite, inexorable, monotonous splendour, a celestial Sahara, crystalline symmetries and harmony, upon which he alone wished to cast a shadow – if you have travelled by plane without taking a nap at the wrong time, then you know the darkness that seems to accompany us – vehement planes, frozen landscapes, frothing, motionless crests, glory. Fragonard surface, someone remarked preciously, and the Good Lord nodded.

Or like a cerebral vortex. That's how much brains I've got for this – for these – he murmured (at this stage of the game). Or a cauliflower. A world-cauliflower. There is in Rome – or there will be: but here it's no use seeing eye to eye with the best minds, who recommend that we remember the future and trust the past seeing how language is Euclidean, and logic is a matter of common law; let the languid efforts of the admittedly impoverished Hungarian verb conjugation remind you of the problematics (to put it politely) of the 'set of all sets'; it's better late than never – so then, there is in Rome, in the Jewish quarter, a tiny *trattoria* that serves a divine *cavalfiore*, and let's not forget the feather-light béchamel, whose fragrance vies with the angels' . . .

The story of the story is simplicity itself, for the necessary condition for a story is time, and the necessary condition for time is death; the Good Lord first had to create death, and to this end he created man. To wit, the Lord created man to be the underling of death. And there's not much one can add to that. It is an interesting trifle that as a rule, men – all men being mortal – do not understand this, or else it dawns on them only gradually. In any case, this is how man became the instrument of the Lord's self-knowledge. (This is God's aforementioned plebeian touch, which gives rise to the angels' – granted, not universal, yet repeated – outbreaks of upper-crust envy. – Apropos Euclid, may I remark tangentially that . . . where shall I begin? . . . that we might consider: the eternal silence of infinite space frightened Pascal half to death, whereas he should have been feeling God's proximity, too; we could say that the language of God is the language of self-love, i.e., of silence, 'where – falling further and further from words – all impurity and incompleteness that besmirch and maim truth cease', for 'ultimate truth simultaneously contains the past, the present, and the future.' But what was I getting at? Oh yes: that the appearance of man signalled the end of this silence, the angels were worried about the Lord's prestige before man, the angels, whose language had been appointed between silence and speech; some describe it as a murmur, others as a howl, a quiet hum or passionate moan. Some equate it with the language of mathematics, especially in view of the growing tendency of mathematics, 'those enormous constructs of form and meaning', to recede from language, the bridges between mathematical symbols and words ever weaker, until they collapse, and the crash – according to some, a gentle swoosh – is the language of angels. Here I am paraphrasing the Anglo-Saxon medicine woman Georgina Stone – not Anna's aunt! – [the chronicler of the historical annihilation and artistic heritage of the *fin de siècle* and the inter-war years in Europe, of the realization and passing of a space-and-time-bound humanism] in Odon Suck's knowing rendition . . .)

With an indulgent smile the Lord awaited the advent of that which must enter into every human life, the realization of death's supreme dominion. This is the point Anna, too, had reached in her prayer: in her eyes astonishment, the astonishment of finitude. For Anna's sake, then, the Lord decided to take up the saxophone. Learn some of those swayin' blues. Not for his salvation – he did not like to meddle in his Father's business – but for a lark, to cheer up this woman.

'Let me make you a roast,' his mother said. No, he wasn't hungry, and besides, he was working, leave him be. He knew that his mother knew that in that case, standing in the kitchen later in the day, he'd spoon into the pot of left-over cold stuffed cabbage, wiping the paprika sauce first on his hand, then his hand on his trousers.

He was well acquainted with the daring essay on the metaphysics of the saxophone by Bella R. S. Sa, the avant-garde New York music critic, which interestingly enough (and possibly not irrespective of the painful path trod by Sa, attention! a man! the child of profligate Puerto Rican parents fleeing to the rich neighbour) grew out of a thesis on 'The Role of the Saxophone in Lukács's Ontology', jumping over its own shadow, as it were, with the motto that has since become famous and infamous in turn: the smallest lukács is greater than the greatest lukács-disciple. (Another essential piece of literature is the pioneering standard, 'The Un-bearable Lightness of the Long Breath [Wind] from Adolphe Sax to Dexter Gordon', by Jaroslav Lae, who has been living in Bottmingen, Switzerland since 1969, and whose nickname, 'the Great *Ach*', was no guarantee against death, referring as it did to the asthma he acquired in a variety of Czech jails.)

In Sa's phrase, the blues knows only how to bury – keeping in mind the archaic custom of certain communities that buried their dead with a dance; thus, for instance, the *siciliano* with its triple asymmetric pulse, originally a mourning dance (Bach: the mezzo aria 'Erbarme Dich' from the St Matthew Passion, and its violin-piano sonata version in C Minor, BWV 1017), which Spanish grandees would still perform around the open grave in the sixteenth century. The saxophone as Non-existence? In the beginning was the Word, and in the end the saxie? The saxophone as bi-sexual? The Good Lord waved it off.

And he summoned, after he'd indeed tasted a little of the Transylvanian cabbage (he ate it without sour cream, but let that remain our little secret), the boss man of the seraphim, to give him some saxophone lessons.

They could not come to terms.

'Pedantic old fool,' raged the Lord, who looked with disgust at the floppy, never resting mouth – because, like all trumpeters, the boss man of the seraphim kept his lips in constant training.

Thereupon the Lord called unto him the pick of the saxophone players. Money no object. A strange epidemic broke out on Earth. The great saxophone players came from far and wide (some, like Chekasin, were sent back to Vilnius, and Laederach to Fertőràkos, Dansco who knows where), Johnny Hodges, Earl Bostic, Tab Smith with the hat,

Hawkins, Sonny Stitt, Art Pepper, Arthur Blythe, Illinois Jaquet, Joe Alexander from Cleveland, Benny Carter, Lester Young (minimal art!), Sonny Rollins, who at night practised on the Williamsburg Bridge and conversed with foghorns; the great Dexter Gordon (did he come back?), and the eccentric Albet Ayler, fished out of the East River at the Congress Street pier of the Brooklyn Bridge (there could be no doubt, the telltale grey tuft on his chin).

The Lord chose Charlie Parker (address courtesy of J. Cortazar). When he came before the Lord the Bird's face still retained the smile (he laughed to himself, as always) at a joke he heard on the Dorsey Brothers' TV show, when death tapped him, as we say, on the shoulder, on 12 March 1955. Charlie Parker called the Lord Bruno.

'Hi, there! Our friend Bruno is as faithful as asthma.' The Lord took out a pack of Gauloises; the bottle of rum he kept in reserve.

'It's been some time,' said the Lord, overcome with emotion.

'You always worry about time. The first, the second, the third, the twenty-first of the month. You stick a number on everything.' Charlie laughed out as only he knew how, full mouth, from somewhere behind his teeth and lips. 'I lost my axe.'

'How could you lose it?' A bad question.

'On the subway. Just to make sure, I put it under the seat. I felt good, I knew it was there, under my feet, safe and secure . . . It was one of the baddest axes in my life. Doc Rodriguez had played on it, you could tell, gone way out of shape, soulwise. The mechanics was all right, but Rodriguez could mess up a Stradivari, just by tuning it.'

By then, nobody dared lend Charlie an instrument, because he would either lose it or instantly wreck it. In Bordeaux he lost Louis Rolling's axe and the one Dedee had loaned him for his English tour he smashed into three pieces, battered, stomped on it. Who knows how many instruments he'd lost, broken, or hocked. And on each he played as only a god can play the alto saxophone, provided he'd given up the lute and the flute beforehand. At least, that's how I see it.

That's why he was here. Now the Lord pulled out the bottle of rum, it was as if someone had turned on the light: surprised, Charlie's grin stretched from ear to ear, teeth gleaming. They drank. Parker had a short fuse as a pedagogue, but he demonstrated the basics. He shouted explanations, waved his arms, made faces. It all showed a certain disregard. Unoffended, the Lord paid close attention.

'Bruno! This is zilch! Zilch-zilch. Zilcher than zilch. Zilch like this don't exist, I can't believe it! Forget your lungs, will you? From the gut, man!' He sighed deeply in the meantime, a man nearing the end of his tether. 'Hold it down! Anticipate! . . . The fingering, Bruno! What're you doing?! Steal, steal the fingering . . . Go on . . . Pull yourself into that tube! . . . Bite! Don't suck, bite! Don't honk, bend that note, what're you doing again?! jump that octave, Bruno! go with the harmony! jump, for the love of God!'

'Hey!' snorted the Lord.

'Bruno, I can't believe this! . . . What are your hands made of?!'

'I must ask you, Bird, don't shout at me.'

'How in God's name do you expect . . .'

'See? That's what I mean.'

'All right, Bruno, take it easy . . . Don't think about anything, drop all your ideas . . . Ideas must come from the instrument, real ideas are instrumental in nature . . . First we go through all the marches . . . then all the house-party standards . . . you gotta know all that virtuso shit . . .

backwards and forwards, from the gut, Bruno . . . nobody said it's a sinch, spiritual quality plus warmth . . . you gotta tear time apart . . .'

The Lord knew this would happen: trouble. He'd met few men with such a passion for anything that had to do with time . . . It happened in Cincinnati, well before the Paris tour, back in '49 or '50. Charlie was in great form then, and the Lord went to the rehearsal expressly to hear him and Miles Davis. They all played with spirit, were satisfied and well dressed, glad to play, no trace of impatience, and the recording engineer waved his approval from behind the small window, like a blissful baboon. And just at the point when Charlie was practically afloat with joy, he quit playing, punched somebody in the nose, and said, 'I'm playing this tomorrow.' The guys froze, two or three played a few more bars, like a train coming to a slow stop, while Charlie kept beating his head and repeating. 'I've already played this tomorrow, it's awful, Miles, I've already played this tomorrow.'

'Whereas I'm quite content with absolute space and time,' the Lord remarked.

'Come now, Bruno. Space and time, they're just words for expressing your own point of view, Bruno! Right? We're talking about your point of view, Bruno! Matter or energy?! What's the difference, Bruno?! Heh?'

They drank, and then Charlie began to talk in a soft voice, did the Lord know what a mortagage was, must be something awful, because whenever his old man mentioned the mortgage, his ma tore at her hair, and they'd end up fighting, really, so that time was unending back home, but music raised him above time, or if the Lord wanted to know what he really felt, he'd have to say that music placed him in time, but then they'd have to assume that this time had nothing to do . . . how should he put it? . . . with them. And that time was squeezing him in on all sides, because it's not a sack you can cram full of stuff.

'If only I could live, always, like when I play, Bruno . . . Have you any idea how much can be jammed into a minute and a half? . . . And then we could live for centuries, and not just me, but Dedee, you, and all the guys; if we found the key, we could live a thousand times longer than we're doing now, in this madness of hours, minutes and tomorrows . . . Listen, Bruno, let me show you something, Bruno . . . You gotta coax that sadness out of the alto, it won't come by itself, you gotta get to your knees, Bruno, you gotta beg, see?! . . . You know what I call this? The "slow death" tempo . . . Blowing the axe is same as singing . . .'

'You lost the tube.'

'Keep your cool, Bruno, it's right here in my hand, invisible . . .'

He measured the Lord up and down real slow, then broke into 'Amoroso', the theme from the Alamo, his legs flung apart, as if he were standing on a swaying ship . . . growled only from the back of the throat, creating rough throaty sound effects, whereupon the instrument wailed like a wounded man, it roared and gasped for air, as 'Errol' Henderson would say; he improvised like the wind, moving quickly, hovering at times, at times swaying back and forth, with sounds that went straight to the centre of the earth, or soared until by sheer force they swept the clouds from the sky.

No use. The Lord had foreseen ('foreseen') that this would happen ('happen'). No use, because for music you didn't need money, or an instrument, or talent, for music you needed – first and foremost – time. And eternity is not time. Infinity is not a quantity. The nonstop nagging was about to begin.

This is the place for the story, he thought, this is the place for a commercial. It's done. Story? Questions. What's the story? Is there one story? Are all stories mine? Is only that story mine in which I change? In a visionary way, as was his bad habit, he understood his enemies, the hatred, too, the anger that could flare up so unexpectedly out of love; he understood the betrayals, the raging envy (and cast a gentle glance at the overweening builder's apprentice from Ulm); he wanted everyone's love, he recalled that Einstein had also been born in Ulm. To see a story and to be in it, wasn't that a contradiction? He glanced at the writer without becoming any wiser. Still, he did not wish to resign himself to that. What could he do, he who was omnipotent? Nothing, He concluded with melancholy, above and beyond everything, nothing. Nothing, nothing, nothing. 'That temperamental lady, Hurricane Lucy, swept past Miami.' He savoured this antiquated conception of himself, this Zeus-paraphrase. I can cast my shadow before me. Nothing is interesting from a distance; from up close it's interesting, from afar, it's beautiful. To be near, to be far.

Suddenly, Parker gave a blast on his saxophone that wrecked the heavenly harmony and desisted. The Lord was a little afraid of him. (By now, Charlie 'Bird' Parker was an angel, of course.) And thereupon the Lord beheld Charlie throw off the blanket that had covered him, and he beheld him in his nakedness, sitting in an easy chair with one leg drawn up, chin to knee, shivering and laughing, naked as the day he was born, on that filthy easy chair.

'It sure is hot,' Charlie said. 'Bruno, check out this cute little scar between my ribs.'

By now they knew each other pretty well, and a naked man is just a naked man, but the Lord was sorely put out: what was he to do so they wouldn't think that Charlie's behaviour had shocked him. Needless to say, Charlie was well aware of this and roared with laughter and kept his leg drawn up in an unseemly manner so that his genitals hung draped over the edge of the chair, like a monkey's at the zoo. His thigh sported suspicious spots, which filled the Lord with unutterable disgust. He quickly covered up Charlie, but he went on laughing, and was clearly very pleased.

'Don't rush it, Bruno. Six months ago. *Six, sax, sex*. Highly ingenious, Bruno. The devil take you, Bruno . . . That tin horn is divine . . . Just now it felt like I was making love, playing on it . . . Don't be jealous, play with more nonchalance . . .'

'What should I play?'

'Play what you believe in. Make music that needs you. Don't pant, let the instrument do the panting. That tube should just wheeze in your hands. Like a tiny creature, let it pant, enjoy the heat. A birdie. Ornithology. And more nonchalance.' He laughed. '*And the truth goes marching on . . .*'

The Lord looked into Charlie Parker's eyes from up close. Where had he seen this horror before except in the mirror, where had sadness, shivering and knowledge looked back at him this way, sharing that glance by turns, adding to the conquered territories, then losing them again? Yes, he'd spend hours in that small corner of the Kunsthistoriches in Vienna where the self-portraits hang, studying the glances, the eyes. In them he recognized his mother's and his own. It was Rembrandt that showed him, showed that he had inherited his mother's glance. That tiny white speck of paint slapped on there, that's what told the whole story. The Good Lord loved matter, he could afford the self-indulgence. Brains *cavolfiore*, milk, Fragonard. Charlie Parker, the ailing angel.

My eternity, he thought. The turtle's. The infinitude of

time until Achilles catches up. There is always a witness. Where had he heard that before?

*

> 'You may go home now. Thank the rabbi from
> Janow. He found some vague reference in
> Moses Maimonedes, that speaks for you.'
> I.B. Singer, *Gimpel the Fool*

'*Über allen Gimplen ist Ruh.*' Silence reigns above the half-wits. Heaven is above, above the clouds. Silence reigned supreme. His mother had dozed off in the easy chair with a book in her lap; he carefully removed the reading glasses from her nose and covered her with the blanket placed there beforehand. Sleep, mother, sleep. Mankind was asleep down below (if we ignore the fact that the earth is round).

His eyes were killing him, wind in the offing. Storm warnings at Lake Balaton, the temperature of the lake at Siófok seventy degrees. Seventy degrees: an attractive but muddled approach to things. He remembered that once Jo Jones from Count Basie's band threw his choke cymbals at Parker, whose music he could not understand. Parker ran out, weeping. He had the battered bakelite saxophone brought up from under the subway seat, 'It's no Selmer, Bruno, but f..k it, I broke it in.' A certain Mr Mizera, the chief cook at the Hotel Imperial at Ostrava, washed down ten mugs in three minutes, this is the world record right now. 'Always looking into things,' he let St Thomas say. He was peevish. He even forgot to eat. He waited for Hrabal to feed his cats, then called to him.

161

THE LORD: *Pane doktore, s Vámi to dlouho nepotravá*, i.e, you can't last much longer, *doktore*.

HRABAL: *Já jsem ten, který platí*, i.e., he's the one who will have to pay up, on his face *reelní hruza*, real terror.

THE LORD: We got your text mixed up. It's you, sir, who should be saying, I won't last much longer, at which I, *reelni hruza*, and pay up!

HRABAL: *Dobře miněno*, i.e., he meant well.

THE LORD: *Či ne tak docela právdu*, i.e, that is not entirely true, but to tell the truth, I don't follow – entirely.

HRABAL: *Jen strach o Vás* . . . ie, it's fear of the Lord.

THE LORD: (remains silent)

HRABAL: *Ani jediné slovo, které by nebylo velmi dobře* uváženo, i.e., there's not a single word he hadn't chewed over a thousand times – supposedly.

THE LORD: (remains silent)

HRABAL: *To mně rozbolelo*, i.e., this pains him no end.

THE LORD: *Škatule, škatule, hejbejte se*, i.e., this is very much like the children's game of musical chairs.

HRABAL: *Tak?*

THE LORD: *Jste žid?* i.e., is he Jewish?

HRABAL: *Nechápu*, i.e., he doesn't follow.

THE LORD: *Ano maš pravdu, mám ho ráda*, i.e., yes, that's right, she loves him, but whom is a mystery, but above all, he can't see what this has to do with the Jews? One *mitzveh* does not a summer make. (According to one irresponsible remark, the Lord himself is one-third Jewish, maybe that's what this refers to. But it's best not to get involved in this. In any case, *mazel tov*.)

HRABAL: *Dvoje šaty mám a přece slušně vypadám*, i.e., the great Czech writer has only two suits, yet he still looks smashing, i.e., he is garbed in the robes of love.

THE LORD: *Krásná vůbec nikdy, vážně vypadám*, i.e., though

truth is one, her faces are many, she could never get top grades for beauty, not really, though sometimes she is attractive enough.

HRABAL: (remains silent)

THE LORD: *Nechat člověka čekat*, i.e., to keep someone waiting; he surely must be thinking that that is not a very nice thing to do.

HRABAL: *Že vlastně Ty jsi člověk, který nemá tušeni o tom*, i.e., the Lord is the one person in the world who can't possibly have the slightest inkling of what that means – a rash statement, if ever there was one.

THE LORD: *Tajemné*, mysterious, i.e., enigmatic.

HRABAL: *Marně*, no use.

THE LORD: *Ženy nepotřebují mnoho*, i.e., women don't ask for much, but what has that got to do with anything?

HRABAL: *Váha světa*, i.e., women are the touchstones of the universe.

THE LORD: *Samozřejmě*, i.e., he is in vehement agreement.

HRABAL: *Čekáš, až to Tobě bude nutné*, i.e., the Lord has a habit of waiting until it suits *him*.

THE LORD: *Nemluvně, pro sebe*, i.e., every babe in arms knows that, as far as it goes, *telegrafovat Ti ten falešný telegram nemá tedy smyslu, neposílám ho*, i.e., it's no use sending false telegrams, pseudo-telegrams, back and forth, and he's not.

HRABAL: *Strach, touha, strach, touha, strach, touha*, fear, yearning, as in desiring someone, fuck your little cooch to shreds, sister-in-law!

THE LORD: *To je krása, to je krása!* Oh, how beautiful! twice.

HRABAL: (remains silent)

THE LORD: *Jsi můj*, you are mine.

HRABAL: (remains silent)

THE LORD: *Nechci, abys na to odpovídal*, i.e., this does not call for an answer.

HRABAL: (he answers, he remains silent)

THE LORD: *Nemáte síly milovat*, i.e., none of you has the strength to love.

HRABAL: (remains silent)

THE LORD: *Nebude toho nikdy*, i.e., it will never happen, there's no knowing what it is. And the *Jste žid*, that was just a joke, but nobody understands it, everybody's paralysed, like Szeicz's horse. (Probably folklore.)

HRABAL: (remains silent)

THE LORD: And what's with the *bubácká kniha*, the book of ghosts?

HRABAL: *O mně rozbil*, i.e., did you break it, perhaps?

THE LORD: Have you bathed in the Malše?

HRABAL: (very softly) I have not done so, but the plum harvest will be exceptional this year.

THE LORD: That's no answer, son, that's just the truth.

His mother snorted in the easy chair. She won't believe that she snores, maybe no one who snores believes that they snore, and his mother none too gently, either; he remembered the saxophone again, mother's alto! he went *tsk-tsk*, she stopped, it always surprised him that this worked. So then, the plum harvest will be exceptional this year. That's something, at any rate.

He looked down at Ulm, to see how the tower was progressing. He saw Staircase Jacob climb up, he sees me, too, as panting, dishevelled, I rest, cold sweat running down my back and forehead, he sees what I'm thinking, everything that I have forgotten by now and do not wish to conjure up in my fantasies, he saw everything simultaneously, the sea of space, the current of time, the branches of a rose bush, the Black Forest and the Black Sea, John Hus and a fatal typo in a grade B novel, the battle of Thermopylae, the flames of Jan Palach and the birth of a little boy called Marcell, then the same little boy's foot-fungus, he saw the entry of the Soviet tanks into Prague, Budapest, Moscow and San Diego, he saw a travelling salesman from Harry Karel Klofanda and Co., an industrious ovule, a corpse with a fly in the public cemetery in Munich, a complex sentence about man's defiant solitude, a lock-jaw, a hammock 'with zero-mileage on it', a wicker chair in a garden, a deckchair that's been left outside, he sees me standing in the sun, Fermi's nuclear reactor and the Ganyelin Trio, Ganyelin at the piano, Tarasov at the drums, his bad left foot, the diminutive Chekasin playing two saxophone mouthpieces at the same time, his cast iron (!) clarinet, he saw Thomas Mann listening to French chamber music after dinner and reading *Die neue Weltbuhne*, Heinrich is writing about Hitler's latest speech in such an amusing way, he saw the famous slow movement of Beethoven's last piano sonata, *Op. 111*, which has a surprising, quick section, decidedly like an advance on the boogie-woogie ('Beethoven heard into the future,' expression courtesy of Sa), he saw John Coltrane's astonishingly long fingers, the blueish hours of dawn (*Les Heures Bleues*), Luther's favourite drink, beer from Einbeck, water cannon in Kaprovka Street, he saw the writer, he saw me, the speeches of János Kádár, Rudoph II masturbating two weeks before his death ('masturbation which – though it may never get you anywhere, nevertheless creates a universal space-time, the genesis of all creation; it is not rhythm, but throbbing!'), all the pebbles that can possibly be found on earth and separately that certain one from Rhodes, he saw every tree and separately that certain blue one, every plain and separately the Hungarian flatlands, every birthday cake and separately those of the woman with purple hair from Morocco, he saw every sentence that has ever been written or held back and separately one: 'They executed your uncle today'; he saw picturesque Hódmezővásárhely and picturesque Mondsee and all the Spanish women, resting his eyes on those who had gotten tired 'just at that moment', he saw the Italian jackets, the light shoes, and *antipasti*, he had a soft spot for the Italians, it's telling that for instance he considered the French Platini an Italian, he saw Glenn Gould humming into the sound recording he was making, he saw Satan, who was playing solitaire, he saw Jacob's face again, me at the 526th step, he saw a carp just under Neu-Ulm, then the same carp at ancient Regensburg, and the same carp again, breaded, on an Austrian plate, with burnt potato slices, not that good crisp type, mind you, but sooty, he saw Anna's mother as a young girl, he saw Bohumil Hrabal's mother as a young woman, he saw the writer's mother at the age of eighteen, wearing a Hungarian folk dress, he saw a thrush, whistling, few-few fatal-few call-*adio*-few, he saw the writer, he saw Anna and the sentence that except for him no one saw, which contained the words writer and Anna, and he saw himself. The tower was progressing well.

He saw everything, and this made him as lonely as my little finger. Solitude (sole etude) is sublime, solitude is misery. There's the rub. Like resin from the bark of a pine tree is time discharged from solitude. Or like when we grab a handful of sour cabbage, and the liquid runs through your fingers, like that. And there are other similes as well.

Carefully, the Lord picked up Charlie Parker's axe. Fingers in line, support, guts, circulation, embouchement, he kept repeating what he'd learned. He had butterflies in his stomach. (He had no ear for music, the most irrefutable proof of which is Bach. The Lord created Johann Sebastian Bach to perfect himself.) Silence reigned. One last glance at our favourite Ulm, hey, there I am! there! me! there! at the top of the tower, dizzy, I lean against the wall, the strong gusts of wind beating against my hair, and there's just one thing in my head, fear, or rather, anxiety, lest the wind sweep my glasses away; anxiously, I grab them tight, *strach, touha*; nauseated, I close my eyes, my eyes are closed, it's at this point that the stone tracery breaks under Jacob's grip, the last stone tracery.

I have five more minutes, the Lord thought, glancing at the young face with its expression of hatred, one, two, th . . . let's go, what're you waiting for . . . He bit the mouthpiece and blew into the tube, he knew right away it was no good, like blowing his nose, universal snot, hopelessly bad, not a little or a lot, but fundamentally, yet he kept blowing on it, no holds barred, determined, with the obstinate vigour of the dilettante, his lungs hurt as if he'd blown them out of his chest, in tatters, bronchus after bronchus, out through the convoluted flute, bloody little clouds fluttering away . . .

He sat distressed and alarmed, a frightened child, the saxophone hanging between his knees. His mother was tiptoeing behind him with that maddening tact that only mothers know how. She stopped behind her son, ran her fingers through his hair, but was afraid to speak because she had been properly intimidated, as she should be. Don't take it to heart, son. She sat down next to him, alighting gently, like an autumn leaf, softly guiding her son's head into her lap. Fidgeting, he looked for some other place to rest it. From time to time, a quiver ran through his frame.

'Love,' he murmured vacuously – and who knows how many times he'd said this before – 'let *me* take care of love.'

The off-key sound crashed mightily throughout the universe, filling every nook and cranny, reaching every distant bay, this off-key, this crude, this inept, merciless and awful saxophone sound, more of a wheeze and a rattle than

167

music, the admission of its own failure, a choking sob, a supplication – this sated the entire created world, this last, resounding word of the novel, this horrible and horribly botched, this banal, frightful, bad, expiatory note, this piece of ineptitude, uniqueness and wholeness.